JUN - - 2014

On Her Way

Stories and Poems About

GROWING UP GIRL

On Her Way

Stories and Poems About

GROWING UP GIRL

EDITED BY **Sandy Asher**

Dutton Children's Books ℮ *New York*

North Lake County
Public Library District
P.O. Box 820
Polson, MT 59860

Copyright © 2004 by Sandy Asher

"A Girl Like Me" copyright © 2004 by Angela Johnson
"The Day Joanie Frankenhauser Became a Boy" copyright © 2004 by Francess Lantz
"The Story Quilt" copyright © 2004 by Robin Michal Koontz
"Rabbit Stew" copyright © 2004 by Marion Dane Bauer
"The Boys in the Bushes" copyright © 2004 by Sonya Sones
"The Palazzo Funeral Parlor" copyright © 2004 by Marthe Jocelyn
"Bird" copyright © 2004 by Margaret Peterson Haddix
"New World Dreams" copyright © 2004 by Elaine Marie Alphin
"Twelve" copyright © 2004 by Donna Jo Napoli
"Flying Free" copyright © 2004 by June Rae Wood
"The Apple" copyright © 2004 by Linda Sue Park
"Annie's Opinion" copyright © 2004 by Sheila Solomon Klass
"Princess Isobel and the Pea: A Love Story in Five Chapters" copyright © 2004 by
   Valiska Gregory
"The Makeover" copyright © 2004 by Bonny Becker
"Girlfriends" copyright © 2004 by Sara Holbrook
"Where the Lilacs Grow" copyright © 2004 by Pamela Smith Hill
"This Is the Way It Is" copyright © 2004 by Miriam Bat-Ami
"The Secret Behind the Stone" copyright © 2004 by Sandy Asher
"Emily Canarsie Has Something to Say" copyright © 2004 by Sue Corbett
"The Wind Will Know Your Name" copyright © 2004 by Patricia Calvert
"Un/titled" copyright © 2004 by Edwidge Danticat

Library of Congress Cataloging-in-Publication Data

On her way: stories and poems about growing up girl/edited by Sandy Asher.—1st ed.
   p. cm.
Contents: A girl like me / by Angela Johnson—The day Joanie Frankenhauser became a boy / by Francess Lantz—The story quilt / Robin Michal Koontz—Rabbit stew / by Marion Dane Bauer—The boys in the bushes / by Sonya Sones—The Palazzo Funeral Parlor / by Marthe Jocelyn—Bird / by Margaret Peterson Haddix—New world dreams / by Elaine Marie Alphin—

Twelve / by Donna Jo Napoli—Flying free / by June Rae Wood—The apple / by Linda Sue Park—Annie Oakley's opinion / by Sheila Solomon Klass—Princess Isobel and the pea: a love story in five chapters / by Valiska Gregory—The makeover / by Bonny Becker—Girlfriends / by Sara Holbrook—Where the lilacs grow / by Pamela Smith Hill—This is the way it is / by Miriam Bat-Ami—The secret behind the stone / by Sandy Asher—Emily Canarsie has something to say / by Sue Corbett—The wind will know your name / by Patricia Calvert—Un/titled / by Edwidge Danticat.

ISBN 0-525-47170-7

1. Girls—Literary collections. [1. Girls—Literary collections. 2. Sex role—Literary collections. 3. Individuality—Literary collections.] I. Asher, Sandy.

PZ5.O54 2004

810.8'092827—dc22   2003049251

Published in the United States by Dutton Children's Books,
a division of Penguin Young Readers Group
345 Hudson Street, New York, New York 10014
www.penguin.com

Designed by Gloria Cheng
Printed in USA • First Edition
10 9 8 7 6 5 4 3 2 1

To Jazmine Hyde,
who is on her way to achieving her dreams,
and to the caring hearts
at CASA of Southwest Missouri

Contents

Welcome to the Celebration!

As an author of books and plays for young people, I've visited schools from Alaska to Florida, and I've met a lot of girls who remind me of someone very familiar—*me*, when I was their age. Sometimes they find a moment to talk to me in private. Sometimes they hand me a note, write me a letter, or send an e-mail. They talk about feeling "different." They tell me they worry about not "fitting in."

"It was okay to be smart in elementary school," says Debbie Palermo, the narrator of my book *Things Are Seldom What They Seem.* "In junior high, smart went out. Pretty and popular came in. Due to circumstances beyond my control, I stayed smart."

She was speaking for me.

That's the first of two reasons I wanted to create this book: Often, characters in stories and poems can talk about tough subjects more easily than real people.

All through elementary school, I was unstoppable: I wrote, directed, and performed plays with my friends; I ran for class president every year (and even got elected now and then); I made friends with girls and boys, and if anyone picked a fight with me, I fought back!

Then my family and I moved. I began seventh grade with all new classmates, and, as Debbie says, everything changed. The things I was good at didn't seem to matter anymore. Rather than risk not "fitting in," I became very quiet.

I stopped. Stopped being *me.*

And I thought I was alone.

Now I know better.

That's the second reason I've gathered these twenty-one stories and poems. I want to show girls like those I've met all across this country that "different" is *okay.* In fact, it's cause for celebration!

I want them to know that trying to "fit in" with the pretty/popular fantasy figures that are thrown at us all day, every day—in school, on TV, in the movies, and in magazines—isn't nearly as important as finding your own real-life hopes and dreams.

I want them to stay unstoppable!

And I want them to know they're not alone.

The young women in this book are on the move: They sail to the New World. They trek the Oregon Trail. They dash through the woods, start over in new cities and towns (and, in one case, a new palace!), and saunter proudly past tall buildings to the ocean.

Their clothing and customs may differ from year to year, but many of their challenges remain the same. Unfairness and cruelty threaten. Loved ones are lost. Hopes and plans are uprooted. Families squabble. Chores never stop needing to be done. Brothers and sisters tease. Friendships often prove try-ing—and, more often, true.

Growing up has never been easy, but these girls tackle it with gusto. As they travel through the American landscape, past and present, in their stories and poems, they seek indepen-dence, adventure, knowledge, justice, and understanding. And, in doing so, they find their own courage and strength.

Like you, these young women have work to do, dreams to dream, and important discoveries to make and to share. They are *on their way.*

Please join us in this celebration of their invincible spirit—and your own!

—Sandy Asher

On Her Way

Stories and Poems About
GROWING UP GIRL

A Girl Like Me

by Angela Johnson

I always dream
I'm flying in Supergirl
underwear
way
up
high,
with everybody I know
saying
"A girl like you shouldn't be
flying
up
there
in
your
underwear."

I used to dream
I walked over tall buildings
in flowing scarves and a cowgirl
hat.
Never was scared or paid
attention when people
I knew said, "A girl like you needs to stop

walking over those tall buildings
in funny clothes and
get down here with
the rest of us."

Once I dreamed I swam
the ocean
and saw everything deep,
cool
and was part of the waves.
I swam on by the people
onshore
hollering,
"A girl like you needs to
stay out of the water
and be dry,
like everyone else."

So . . .
Yesterday
I bought
a cape and more hats,
borrowed some scarves
from my mom
and walked past
tall buildings
to the ocean,
'cause a girl like me
should always be
thinking

way up
high
and making
everything
better than
the dream.

The Day Joanie Frankenhauser Became a Boy

by Francess Lantz

7:06 A.M.

I'm pulling a T-shirt over my head when I hear Mom's voice, all pinched and disapproving. "You're wearing *that* on your first day of school?"

"What?" I ask, shaking my short hair into place.

"Look at yourself. You look like a boy."

I frown, then walk to the bathroom to gaze at myself in the mirror. I'm wearing a skateboarding T-shirt and shorts. My hair's a little mussed, but other than that I look normal, just the way I always look.

"I wish you had a big sister," Mom said, sighing. "Maybe you'd listen to her."

I shrug and walk into the kitchen. Mom never used to criticize how I look. But lately she's been bringing home all kinds of lame, girly-girl clothes and suggesting I wear them to school. As if! I mean, what am I supposed to do at recess? You can't dribble a basketball in a pink dress and plastic sandals.

"I just thought you'd want to look nice on your first day," Mom says, pouring me a glass of orange juice.

My stomach does a double-dribble. Here I am, about to start fifth grade in a new school, a new town, a new state even. I don't want to think about it.

"I do look nice," I mutter.

But I'm starting to wonder.

8:15 A.M.

"Ernesto Ardo?"

"Here."

"Miranda Bennett."

"Here."

I look around, trying to figure out who I might want to make friends with. Or—since I'm the new kid in a class where everybody has probably known each other since kindergarten—who might want to make friends with *me*. A boy with curly brown hair and freckles looks my way and smiles.

Good. I was expecting only the girls in the class to show any interest in me. But it's the boys I'm interested in—unless there's a girl here who's into basketball, skateboarding, and ice hockey. And how likely is that?

"Gary Dilliplane," the teacher calls.

"Here," the freckle-faced boy answers.

I smile back and wonder if he plays basketball.

"Kellie Epstein."

"Here."

"John Frankenhauser."

I open my mouth, then freeze. Did she say *John?*

"John is new to our school," the teacher says. "He just moved here from Colorado. John, where are you?"

I feel confused, flustered. *There must be a typo on the attendance sheet,* I want to say. *My name is Joan. Everyone calls me Joanie.*

But then I think, what if I said "here"? It's crazy, I know, but the truth is I've always wondered what it would be like to be a boy. Then I could wear the clothes I like without my mom giving me a hard time and ride my skateboard without everyone calling me a tomboy. The way I see it, boys have it easy. They don't have to dress up or stay clean or sit quietly—not the way girls do, anyway—and no one expects them to know how to cook or sew or comfort a blubbering baby. It sounds pretty good to me.

All these thoughts flash through my mind in less than a second. And suddenly, before I even know what's happening, I raise my hand and say, "Here."

I wait for the teacher to squint at me and cry, "Wait a minute, you're a girl!" But all she says is, "Welcome to Vista Elementary, John."

I can't believe this is happening! What have I done? I stare down at my desk, my face burning, and mutter, "Thanks."

There's no turning back now.

10:45 A.M.

The bell rings and Ms. Moodley says, "Line up for recess."

I stand up on shaky legs. For the last two-and-a-half hours, Ms. Moodley has been talking about what we're going to learn this year. She's given us reading and math comprehension tests to—as she put it—"refresh our memories and get us all in a fifth-grade state of mind." Then she read us the first chapter of a book called *Frindle*.

Through it all I've been in a state of quiet hysteria. I keep glancing around at the boys in my class, trying to do exactly what they do. It's weird. In the past, I never thought about how I sit or what I do with my hands. I just did what came naturally. Now I'm careful to keep my knees apart, to crack my knuckles every couple of minutes, to guffaw rather than giggle.

I'm certain it's just a matter of time until someone figures out I'm an imposter, but as we walk to the playground, Gary comes up to me and says, "Ms. Moodley told me to show you where the boys' room is."

Oh my gosh! I hadn't thought of that. I decide right then and there to never go to the bathroom again.

"It's over by the water fountain," Gary says, pointing. "Hey, do you play basketball?"

"Sure," I reply. I don't have to lie about that. I'm pretty good. But at my old school, the boys never let me join their game. If a teacher forced them, they refused to pass me the ball. I tried to start a girls' game, but I couldn't find enough kids who wanted to play. So usually I just shot baskets by myself.

"Watch out for Zane," Gary says as we join a group of boys on the blacktop. He points to a tall, muscular kid with a blond buzz cut. "He plays for keeps."

Zane spots me. "Who are you?" he asks.

"Jo—John," I stammer.

"He's new," Gary explains.

"Tell me something I don't know." Zane turns away. "I choose José, Kristian, and Eric. Let's play."

I glance around, waiting for someone to argue, but nobody

does. Zane goes out of bounds and tosses the ball to Kristian. Kristian passes to Eric. Out of the corner of my eye, I see Zane slide under the basket. I run over to guard him.

"Eric, here," he calls.

Eric passes. I reach out to grab the ball, but suddenly I feel a sharp pain in my ribs. I stagger sideways and fall to the blacktop. Through teary eyes, I watch Zane make the basket.

"Doesn't count," I call. "You elbowed me."

Zane looks down at me. "Are you crying?" he asks with a smirk.

"No, I just—"

"Need a Kleenex?" José asks, all fake concern.

"No, he wants his blankie," Eric scoffs.

Gary holds out a hand to help me up. "Come on," he says, "let's play."

What else am I going to do? Tell a playground monitor and spend the rest of my days at Vista Elementary being called a tattletale? I jump to my feet and grab the ball.

"Can I play?" a voice asks.

It's a girl. She's taller than Zane, and her red hair is pulled back in a ponytail.

"You again?" Zane asks. "I thought we explained this to you in fourth grade. This is serious basketball. No girls allowed."

"Hey, that's not fair," I blurt out.

The boys turn to stare at me. I'm sure they can read the truth about me in my eyes. But all Zane says is, "Since when do new kids make the rules? Besides, who says it isn't fair? We don't ask the girls to let us braid friendship bracelets with them, do we?"

The boys laugh, Gary included. Then Gary motions for me to throw him the ball. I hesitate, then pass. The girl is left standing there as the game sweeps by her. Out of the corner of my eye, I see her turn and walk away.

"John," Gary calls, "heads up!"

It takes me a second to recognize my name, but I recover and catch the pass. Two dribbles and I'm in the key. But Zane is waiting for me. Our eyes meet, and I know in that instant it's him or me. I set my jaw and step in, shoving Zane hard as I go up for the shot. He grunts and falls back. The ball rolls around the rim and drops in.

My teammates let out a cheer—all except Gary, who's eyeing me with a look I can't quite read. Uncertainty? Disappointment? Or is it respect? He steps forward and holds up his hand for a high five. I slap it and start to smile, but he turns away.

12:00 NOON

I walk through the cafeteria line and out into the courtyard. I'm still thinking about the basketball game and how it felt to shove Zane out of the way. Good, and not good. I liked showing him he couldn't intimidate me. And when the guys cheered, I felt giddy. But it was cheating—an obvious foul. And that felt bad.

But maybe that's the way guys play, I tell myself. Maybe it's expected. My brothers never play that way, but maybe they just go easy when I'm around. I'm not sure anymore.

"John, over here."

It's Zane, sitting at a picnic table with a bunch of guys from the basketball game. I feel good, like I've been accepted. Only it's John they're accepting, not Joanie, and that feels weird.

I sit down between Zane and Eric. "What is this stuff?" I ask, looking down at my plate.

"Fried beaver brains," Eric says.

Some girls would be grossed out, I guess, but not me. "With a side of muskrat guts," I add, taking a bite. "Mm, good."

"Hey, Zane, you playing basketball at the Y this year?" José asks.

"Naw. No time."

"Since when do you not have time for basketball?" Gary asks.

"Since my dad grounded me for breaking his power drill." He shrugs. "I don't care. I've outgrown the Y team. They're still playing baby ball."

I glance at Zane. He doesn't look as happy as he sounds, but nobody questions him on it. They just sit there, shoving food in their mouths. Kristian lets out a resounding burp, and we all laugh.

"There she is," Zane says suddenly.

It's the girl who wanted to join our basketball game. She's walking across the courtyard, swinging her lunch bag.

"How does she expect to play basketball with those two balloons on her chest?" Zane smirks. "They've got to slow her down."

At first, I'm baffled. Then I realize what he's talking about. The girl is wearing a bra beneath her blouse. I can see the outline of the straps. This, by itself, is nothing unusual. Lots of fifth-grade girls (not me, of course, but plenty of others) wear bras, whether they need them or not. I guess they think it makes them look more grown-up and feminine.

But, unlike those girls, this girl really needs it.

"You ever hear of that bird, the blue-footed booby?" Kristian asks. He points at the girl's blue socks. "That's her."

The guys crack up, all except me.

"Hey, Jasmine," Zane calls. "Nice boobies."

The girl blushes. "Shut up."

Zane looks puzzled. "What? Haven't you ever heard of the blue-footed booby? It's a beautiful bird. Long beak, big chest . . ."

Jasmine looks like she's going to cry. She clutches her lunch bag and hurries away.

I want to tell the guys to leave Jasmine alone. I want to tell them she can't help the way she looks, and besides, what's wrong with breasts? All women have them, including every player in the WNBA. Jasmine is just a little ahead of schedule, that's all.

But I'm scared to do anything that might clue the guys in to my secret identity. So I keep my mouth shut.

Zane reaches in his pocket and pulls out a five-dollar bill. "First guy who snaps her bra gets this. Only don't get excited because it's going to be me."

"Come on, man," Gary says. "Leave her alone."

"Leave her alone," Zane mocks in a girlish voice.

"I think Gary likes her," José says.

The guys crack up and Eric begins to sing, "Gary and Jasmine sitting in a tree. K-I-S-S-I-N-G."

Am I supposed to sing along? I don't want to, but Zane is looking at me. Unless I want to blow my cover, I have to fit in, go with the flow. Nervously, I mouth the words.

"Aw, shut up," Gary mutters.

2:06 P.M.

We're sitting in the computer lab, learning how to write a business letter. Gary's at the next computer over. "When you're finished," the teacher says, "you can play a computer game until the bell rings."

"You finished?" Gary whispers.

"Pretty much."

"Well, how do you like Vista so far?"

So far. I try to picture the year ahead. Until this moment, I haven't really thought about the future. I mean, how long can I keep up this boy act? How long do I even want to?

"Okay, I guess," I say. "It was tough leaving my old friends. And now I have to find new ones."

"You've got one already," he says with a smile.

I look into his eyes, and my heart does a funny little rabbit hop. Suddenly, I don't feel like a boy at all. Gary looks at me quizzically. Does he know the truth? My stomach tightens.

"Tell me about the Y basketball league," I say quickly. "It's all boys, right?"

"No, co-ed. There are nine or ten girls. One of them is like five-foot-seven. She's good, too."

"How does Zane feel about that?" I ask with a chuckle.

"How do you think? He hates her." Gary pauses, looks down at his hands. "So, John, you planning on winning that five dollars?"

He's talking about snapping Jasmine's bra. What am I supposed to say? The whole thing makes me sick. But that's not how boys are supposed to feel, is it? I mean, that can't be what Gary feels. So if I let on I think differently, will he mock me? Call me a chicken? Or will he figure out the truth?

Part of me wants that to happen. This masquerade is wearing me out. But if I tell Gary I'm a girl, what will happen? What if he laughs at me? What if he stops being my friend?

"I don't know," I say at last. "How about you?"

"Gary and John," the computer teacher snaps, "I said if you're finished with your work you can play a game. A *silent* game."

Gary turns back to his computer, and I never find out his answer.

2:55 P.M.

School ends and I walk outside. Boy, am I exhausted. I can't wait to go home and just be myself.

"Hey, John," a familiar voice calls. "Over here."

Zane and the rest of the b-ball players are standing under the flagpole. Reluctantly, I shuffle over.

"Jasmine walks home," Zane says. "We're going to follow her and see who can snap her bra first."

I glance at Gary. He's looking down at his Nikes.

"Here she comes," Eric hisses.

Jasmine strolls by, completely unaware of what's about to happen. Zane waits until she gets about fifty feet up the sidewalk. Then he slowly starts after her.

The other boys follow, and I go, too. I tell myself that I'm joining them because I want to look out for Jasmine, help her somehow. But I have to admit that part of why I'm going along has to do with Zane, with the power he has over the boys, over me. He's just that kind of guy. When he tells you to do something, you do it.

We follow for about two blocks, the boys stifling their snickers, until Jasmine cuts across a vacant lot. "Now!" Zane commands and starts running.

Jasmine spins around, sees Zane, and gasps. He overtakes

her, but instead of just snapping her bra, he grabs her and pulls her toward the bushes.

"Stop! Let me go!" she shrieks.

"Zane, are you crazy?" Gary demands. "What are you doing?"

"Long as we're here, let's see what color it is," Zane says with a grin.

Gary hesitates, but the other boys run over to help. Jasmine's wide eyes look around wildly. They meet mine, and she shoots me a pleading look. Does she know? Can she see inside to the real me?

In that instant, I know I can't pretend any longer. "Let her go, Zane!" I shout, sprinting forward. I jump on his back and drag him off her.

We hit the grass and roll. He shoves me off him, then leaps to his feet. "What's the matter with you?" he screams.

"There's nothing wrong with me," I say. "You're the one who's acting like a idiot."

Zane looks disgusted. "I thought you were okay. One of us. But you're a chicken, a total wuss."

"I'm not a wuss," I cry. "I'm a girl!"

Zane couldn't look more surprised if I'd told him I was a vampire. "A *girl*?" he sputters.

"From now on, you can call me Joanie," I say. "Better yet, don't talk to me at all." I turn to Jasmine. "Come on, I'll walk you home."

Jasmine looks almost as stunned as the boys, but when I walk across the grass, she falls into step beside me. We leave the boys standing there. They don't look so tough anymore. They just look confused and—except for Zane, who is readjusting his cocky smile—a little ashamed.

• • •

3:49 P.M.

I explain everything to Jasmine on the way home. She thanks me and asks me in, but I just want to get home. We agree to eat lunch together tomorrow, then I leave.

I start walking down the sidewalk, wondering how I'm going to face Zane and the guys tomorrow. By lunchtime the whole school will know. Man, I'll never live it down.

That's when I see Gary. He's standing at the corner, a sheepish smile on his face.

"Hi," I say.

"Hi." He hesitates, then adds, "Joanie." He kicks a pebble into the street. "Look, I just want to say . . . well, you were incredible back there. I mean, you did something I never had the guts to do. You stood up to Zane."

I can't believe it! He's not laughing at me. He's impressed with what I did. "I'm not so brave," I say. "I just couldn't keep pretending to be some macho dude. That's not me—not even close."

"But this morning, when Ms. Moodley called the roll . . ."

"It was a mistake," I said. "But I decided to go along with it. I wanted to see what it felt like to be a boy. Or at least I thought I did."

He laughs. "So how did it feel?"

I think a moment, then say, "I imagined it would be simpler than being a girl, but it wasn't. I wasn't supposed to cry, wasn't supposed to say what I was really thinking. And when Zane was around, I felt like I constantly had to prove myself."

"I feel that, too," Gary says quietly. "But I'm not like Zane. At least I don't want to be. I mean, isn't there another way?"

"I don't know," I answer. "I'm still trying to figure out what being a girl means. Like do I have to wear makeup and stand around with my friends at recess, gossiping and giggling?"

"I hope not," Gary says, "because I want to play basketball with you."

I snort a laugh. "After today, I don't think Zane is going to let me join the game."

"Who said anything about Zane?" Gary asks. "I was thinking more of some one-on-one."

"Well, okay," I reply, "but don't expect me to go easy on you. I've got a killer hook shot and I plan to use it."

"You're on, Frankenhauser. But first, do you mind if I walk you home?"

"Yeah, I do. But I'd be happy to walk *you* home."

Gary laughs. "Okay, look, how about if we just walk together?"

I nod, and we fall into step, side by side. And then I realize something. For the first time all day, I feel totally happy to be exactly what I am: a girl.

The Story Quilt

by Robin Michal Koontz

"What's that old thing?" I asked.

Mom stroked the huge patchwork quilt in her arms. "Grandie made this," she said. "Imagine that."

"Really," I said. I stared around at all the boxes and piles of musty stuff we still had to go through. I had been ready to run from this chore since we started. Even homework would be better than this.

Mom pressed her face close and sniffed at the old, yucky material and smiled. Gross! I tried not to imagine the mice and rats and whatever else had pooped on the smelly thing since it had been up here in my great-grandmother's attic.

"Look at all the work that went into this," Mom said, holding it up for me. I tried to ignore her as she practically shoved it in my face. All I could think about was how weird it was to be nosing into Grandie's things. Mom was even acting happy about it. Earlier we had gone through boxes and boxes of Grandie's research papers and astronomy books. Mom sorted through tons of letters and journals and had me organize them into file boxes. It didn't seem right. This was Grandie's stuff,

Grandie's house. We had no business being here. I hated the "for sale" sign on her lawn.

"Spread those plastic bags out on the floor," Mom said, and I did as she asked. Then she carefully laid the quilt out on the plastic. Bits of fluff and dust rose and glimmered in the light from the little window where we stood. "See the red pieces in the star shapes here?" Mom pointed at fuzzy red triangles. "Those came from Grandie's old long johns that finally wore out after about thirty years."

What are long johns? I wondered. I didn't ask, though. Mom was acting like she was in another world. I turned and looked out the window as she knelt down beside the old quilt.

"These blue plaid pieces, they are from my granddad's favorite old hunting shirt. She patched the thing about a hundred times, but it finally went to the scrap box. I remember when he moaned about that." Mom giggled. "And how Grandie laughed at him and kissed his cheek."

The thought of old people kissing was almost as disgusting as that musty old quilt. Would Mom ever shut up?

But no. "Look at the yellow pieces here, and here," she said. "I remember those came from a tablecloth Grandie used for special occasions."

"So why did it end up in the scrap box?" I turned to her and asked, hoping I could get her to finish with her stories and get us out of here. She was sitting cross-legged next to the quilt now, like she planned to stay there all afternoon.

Mom giggled again. "Ah, well, your Uncle Keith and I snuck it out to use for a fort. It got a little beat-up." Then she laughed hard. "Ah, shoot, we were in so much trouble for ruining the Sunday finest!"

It was kind of fun to think about my mom doing something bad. I never heard her say "snuck" in my entire life. Maybe next time she yelled at me, I could bring this up. I began to study all the intricate patterns of colored patches in the quilt. It looked like it was made of hundreds of tiny bits of cloth, maybe even thousands.

"If Grandie were here, she could tell us where every piece of material in this quilt came from," Mom said. "She even used it to remind her of stories, don't you remember?"

And then I did remember. Grandie holding me in her lap, both of us wrapped up in the cozy folds. As Grandie told me a story, her fingers would trace over the patterns. Her voice was warm and soft. She called me Tigger. "Sit still, Tigger," she'd say, "and I'll tell you a story." I quickly brushed the memory away.

"A quilt like this would sell for hundreds of dollars at an antique store, you know." Mom stood and began folding it up again.

"You're going to sell it?" I asked. Sure, I could think of about a dozen things right off the bat we could buy with hundreds of dollars. We never seemed to have enough money to buy anything. . . .

"Oh, don't look at me like that; I'm not going to sell Grandie's quilt," she said. "I'm giving it to you." Then she finished folding it and handed it to me.

"Uh, thanks," I said, reluctantly taking the thing in my arms. It was heavy, and the musty smell was almost too much.

"And don't wash it," Mom warned. "It's fragile. It would just fall apart."

"But Mom," I protested, "maybe you should just sell it. I mean, what am I supposed to do with it?" It felt weird just holding it. The memories tried to come back, like the thing was haunted or something. I shook them off again.

"First we'll hang it outside to air," she said. "Then you'll tuck it in a safe place in your closet. Every change of the season, you'll need to take it out and refold it."

"What for?" I asked.

"So it doesn't wear out at the creases," she said. "It'll hold up longer that way."

"And then what?" I asked.

"Let's put it in the car and get back to work," was all she said.

It was a long drive from Grandie's to our house. Mary, the caregiver, was waiting for us. "She had a bad afternoon, but she's resting now," she told us. "If she wakes up during the night, give her one of these, more if you have to." She handed my mom a bottle of pills.

Grandie had a disease in her brain, was how Mom explained it. It started with a stroke. Then another stroke. Each time she had a stroke, she got worse. First she couldn't drive anymore, then she couldn't walk very well, and then she started doing things like leaving the stove on or forgetting to eat. So Mom got her to move in to our house this summer. Mom and I were the only family Grandie had left. She and I read books and worked jigsaw puzzles together, and sometimes we stayed up late and sat outside to watch the night sky. I liked having Grandie live with us.

But then Grandie had another stroke, a bad one, the doctor said. Now she couldn't do anything for herself, and she didn't seem to know who anyone was. Mom didn't want to send her to a nursing home, so she got Mary to help take care of her.

Mom walked Mary to the door. They whispered to each

other, and then Mary left. Then Mom turned back to me. "Okay, kiddo," she said, "let's get something to eat. I'm starved!" So we made macaroni and cheese from a box and stuffed ourselves with that and corn chips. I almost asked her where the vegetables were but changed my mind.

Later that night I woke up. A dog was howling right outside my window! I jumped out of bed to shut the window, but it was closed and the howling sounds were coming from the bedroom next door—Grandie's room. A dog was in her room? I ran out to get Mom, but she was already coming toward the open door. "Shhhhh," she said when I opened my mouth to talk. "It's Grandie; she's having a bad dream. Go back to bed."

So I went back to my room and shut the door. Then I sat on my bed and listened to Grandie howl like a dog. After a while, she stopped. I listened to my mom's footsteps as she went back to her room. I stayed awake for a long time. I kept thinking about Grandie last month, Grandie last year. Grandie as long as I could remember did not howl like a dog. Grandie looked after me and made cookies and told stories. She was a famous astronomer who wrote books and discovered new stars. Even after her brain got the disease, she could work a jigsaw puzzle faster than anyone. And just two weeks ago, she and I had huddled together in the dark and watched meteor showers blaze through the sky over our backyard.

Early the next morning I tiptoed into Grandie's room. She had all her covers torn off and was lying on her back. Her mouth was moving, and her fingers were fussing with the lace collar of her nightgown. "Grandie?" I said. Her eyes were staring at the ceiling. "Grandie?" I called again. "It's me, Tigger." But Grandie just lay there, her mouth moving with no sounds coming out, her fingers twirling. She still didn't seem to notice me as I backed out of the room.

I checked my mom. She was sleeping. I guess she had been up a lot lately taking care of Grandie. She said it was like having a baby again. I guess it was. I went back to my room and looked at the old quilt lying in the corner. I gathered it up and took it outside. We had a clothesline in the summer because Mom said it saved electricity. I struggled to get the quilt up and over the line and watched it flap in the breeze. It was hard to imagine Grandie making it, at least not the Grandie who lay in bed on her back, staring at the ceiling. The Grandie who didn't even remember who I was.

It took a week for the quilt to smell okay again. I brought it in every night and took it out to the clothesline every morning. That night when I brought it inside, I decided to put it on Grandie's bed. Maybe it would help to calm her. She was already sleeping when I laid it over her. I quickly left the room. It was hard to look at her.

But later that night it was the same as it had been all week. Grandie woke up and started howling. Mom went to her and coaxed her to take the pill and stayed until she got quiet again. I watched from the doorway as Grandie flung the quilt and the sheets to the floor. "You should go," Mom said. "She'll be quiet soon."

I went back to my room and waited until I heard Mom go back to hers. Then I crept out and peeked in at Grandie. The quilt was still on the floor in a heap. I picked it up and spread it back over her. Grandie's eyes were closed, but her hands immediately went to the quilt edge and began stroking the patchwork.

I leaned down close to her face. "Do you remember me now?" I whispered to her. Her mouth moved just a little, and I swear, she smiled, just a little.

Grandie still howled at night sometimes, and on other nights, she was quiet. Sometimes I sat up with her and watched her fingers fuss with the quilt even when she seemed to be sleeping.

But soon, she stopped doing anything at all.

Now I have this quilt that Grandie made and that she used to remember stories. I'm sitting on my bed and remembering the stories Mom told about the red pieces, the plaid pieces, and especially the yellow pieces from the tablecloth. I am trying to remember the stories Grandie told me while I sat in her lap, wrapped up with her in the cozy folds. I was just a little kid then, and it feels like a long time ago.

I remember laughing, so the stories must have been funny. Now that I think about it, I remember one about a brother, or maybe it was a cousin, who always wore suspenders to hold up his baggy pants that were hand-me-downs from his older brothers. One day when they were both kids Grandie snipped off his suspenders from behind, and his pants fell down. He was wearing huge shorts underneath. They were striped like some of the pieces on the quilt.

Now that I think about it, I remember one story about the day the sun disappeared. It was a scary story at first, but Grandie explained about the solar eclipse while she touched bright white and black shapes on the quilt. Then when we had a real solar eclipse, she took me to a planetarium where we watched it from a special telescope. I had forgotten all about that until I held the quilt and let my fingers trace over the patterns, just like Grandie used to do.

Now I'm going to fold up the quilt and put it in my closet where it will be safe. I'll take it out at every change of the season and refold it, so it doesn't wear out at the creases. But I'm also going to take it out when I want to remember Grandie and her stories. Maybe I'll even have a few stories of my own.

Rabbit Stew

by Marion Dane Bauer

The wagon train had been inching forward for weeks, yet months of travel lay before them still. They hadn't even reached Fort Laramie yet, nor Scotts Bluff, nor Chimney Rock. Nonetheless, the entire train had stopped this day for the men to make repairs on some of the wagons, for the women to wash their family's clothes in the Platte River and lay them out to dry in the searing sun, for the children to scatter like burrowing mice through the prairie grass.

Lizzie had spent the morning helping her mother with the laundry and keeping an eye on her younger sisters.

"Watch them close," Mama had said. "If they wander away from the wagon, they will surely be lost in this sea of grass."

Mama never let the little girls out of her sight . . . or Lizzie's. But then, ever since Papa had first decided they were all going to make the long trek to Oregon, it seemed to Lizzie that Mama had been afraid of everything. The cholera and the smallpox that had plagued some of the trains that had gone before. The endlessly turning wagon wheels that could grab and crush a young child. The mountains standing between them and their destination. The Indians whose lands they dared cross.

Lizzie wasn't afraid. Like Papa, she thought traveling from Independence, Missouri, to Oregon City was as grand an adventure as she was ever likely to have. Her only regret was that Mama kept her tied so tightly to her apron strings, watching her little sisters, washing and baking, staying *safe*. And safe she was. So safe she could now bake biscuits in the iron pot dug into the coals of the fire quite as well as Mama. And she had learned to beat and beat their clothes on the river rocks until they came clean. Yet she had never once, in all the weeks they had been on the trail, been farther away from the safety of the covered wagon than a cowboy could spit. Not that she'd had a chance to meet a cowboy yet, either.

She had asked and asked Mama. "The twins can run. Why not me?"

But Mama always said, "You are eleven years old, Lizzie. Too old to be tagging after boys, even if they are your own brothers."

Too old to have any fun at all, it seemed, though Robert and John, a full year older than she, seemed to disappear whenever and wherever they liked.

How Lizzie longed to slip out from under her mother's tireless gaze, just once. This morning would have been a good time. The twins had gone off again, promising to come home with a rabbit for dinner. Though how they were going to bring home a rabbit without Papa's gun was anybody's guess.

Ordinarily Papa would have let them take the gun, but this morning he had said he needed to take it apart to give it a good cleaning. They were, he pointed out, moving ever deeper into Indian country.

So Lizzie wasn't just surprised, she was positively amazed when Robert and John came marching back, their hands empty of rabbits, of course, and asked Mama if Lizzie could join them on their hunt.

"Oh, please, Mama!" she cried, before her mother had a chance even to think the word *no*.

"We need her," John insisted, giggling and elbowing his twin.

For an instant, suspicion tingled in Lizzie's scalp. What was the merriment about? But the whole idea of her brothers actually asking for her company was so unexpected—and so utterly delightful—that she put their jostling and giggling aside. Who ever knew what amused boys, anyway?

Mama straightened slowly from the shirt she'd been scrubbing, her lips set in a thin line. She pressed her work-reddened hands against her back and looked out across the endless grass that danced so invitingly. Then her gaze returned to Lizzie, who had risen from her place on the riverbank, clutching a sodden pair of britches.

Mama sighed. "I can't imagine why you need Lizzie," she said to the boys, "but it's been a long time since she's had a chance for anything like fun. So if you'll watch her close, she may go."

Watch her close! As though the twins, just by being boys, were so much wiser, so much more responsible than she. But Lizzie didn't complain. She didn't want to be caught even *thinking* a complaint.

"Oh, thank you, Mama," she cried, dropping the half-washed britches onto the riverbank. "Thank you! Thank you!" And she flung her wet arms around her mother's neck and turned to run after her brothers without once looking back.

"Don't go far!" their mother called after them. "Remember . . ." But Lizzie was running too fast and the prairie wind was too strong in her ears to hear whatever it was she was supposed to remember.

"What are we going to do?" she asked, breathless, once they had stopped, far from the circled wagons.

"We're going to get us some rabbits," Robert said, his freckled face gleaming in the sun.

"Yankee style," John chimed in.

"And we need you to hold the bag," Robert finished.

"What bag?" Lizzie asked, but even as she spoke, John produced from beneath his shirt a burlap bag that had once held potatoes.

She reached out to take it, but slowly. "What am I supposed to do with this?"

"You're going to catch the rabbits," Robert announced.

John nodded enthusiastically. "And then you'll get to be the one to carry the jacks back to camp and give them to Mama."

The rabbits here on the prairie were called jackrabbits. They were actually a kind of hare, Papa said, but they were long and lean and tall-eared and spent too much time running to make for tender eating. Still, some rabbit stew to go with their beans and rice and biscuits tonight would be welcomed by all—however tough the meat—and the one who brought it back to the wagon would be something of a hero.

"All right," Lizzie said, shrugging away her own skepticism. "What do I do?"

They showed her. They took her to a small ravine, a long, shallow indentation in the flat prairie. Flat as a cracker, Papa said of the prairie, but when you looked closely the endless prairie wasn't as flat as it seemed. There were sinkholes that could open up and claim a whole team with its wagon. There were ruts where wagon after wagon had traveled before them, all on the selfsame journey. And there were ravines, usually covered by the waving grass so that they were hidden until a person—or a pair of oxen—stepped down into them. This one probably carried water when there was enough rain for extra water to be lying about, but now it was perfectly dry and filled with grass and wild-flowers.

"What you do," John explained—he was usually the one who did the explaining—"is to crouch down at the bottom there, fac-ing that way, and hold the bag open."

"For what?" Her suspicions were growing. She had lived with the twins her entire life, and she could usually tell when they were giving her a good tweak.

"To catch the rabbits. What do you think?"

"Do you suppose I'm a ninny?" She let the burlap bag fall limp at her side. "What's going to make jackrabbits run into my sack?"

"*We* are!" It was Robert stepping in this time, and he was practically jumping up and down in his delight at their plan . . . or their joke. Whichever it was.

"We're going to go on up the ravine, and we'll walk back toward you, beating the grass with sticks to make the jacks run down the ravine. When they reach you, they'll be so blind with fear, they'll run right into your sack, and all you'll have to do is close it up to keep them inside."

She knew better. She really did. But it was so unusual for Robert and John to come asking for her company that she didn't want to do or say anything that would prompt them to change their minds. After all, what did she know about catching rabbits? Maybe true Yankees did do it this way.

"Unless," John added solemnly, "you're afraid."

"Of course I'm not," Lizzie said. "I'm never afraid! I'm not like Mama!"

The boys exploded into laughter again at that and poked one another some more, as though she had said something extremely funny. Then they turned and disappeared into the long grass.

So Lizzie, feeling just a bit foolish, crouched in the bottom of the small ravine, facing the way her brothers had gone, held the burlap bag open, and waited.

A feathery purple flower—she didn't know what it was called—tickled her elbow. Her sleeves were still pushed high on her arms from doing the laundry, and she pulled them down, being careful to keep the sack gaping widely as she did. She would have liked to pick the purple flower and take it home to Mama. Mama knew the names of nearly every flower there was, even in this strange new land. If she didn't know the exact name, she knew what other flower it was most like. But taking home a rabbit or two for their evening meal would be better, even, than taking flowers.

A mosquito whined around her head and settled on the back of her neck. When she took one hand away from the burlap bag to slap at it, the bag fell closed. And the whining buzz only grew louder. She took a firmer grip on the sack.

The sun bore down, a weight on her scalp, especially along the part that Mama made so firmly every morning when she braided Lizzie's hair. Lizzie should have been wearing her bonnet, of course, but she had taken it off when she was bending over the river stones, pounding the garments, and had forgotten to put it back on when the boys had called. Mama would scold her for that. Young ladies were supposed to keep their skin—

especially their faces—pale and fine. Lizzie didn't suppose, though, that any of the other "young ladies" who walked beside creaking wagons all the way from Missouri to Oregon City were particularly pale when they arrived. Even Mama's skin was turning a pleasant coppery tone, and there were new gold highlights in her brown hair.

Lizzie's legs were beginning to ache from her awkward position. The boys and the jackrabbits were certainly taking their time!

She shifted her weight from bare foot to bare foot. At first, she had begun the long journey wearing shoes, but seeing how quickly they came to show wear—and knowing that colder, harder country lay ahead—Mama had let Lizzie tuck the shoes away into the trunk and run barefoot the way her brothers did. Still, Mama worried about her going without shoes. She fretted that Lizzie's feet would grow too large from not being properly shod and that she could never be a lady with oversized feet. Lizzie wondered how many "ladies" they would find in Oregon City, anyway.

She didn't say that to Mama, though. Mama had enough to worry about, just following Papa from place to place. The family had already gone with him from southern Indiana to Illinois and then on to Missouri. Papa never seemed to be content for long, wherever they settled. This time, Mama said, they would have to stay. If they went any further west than Oregon, they would all be swimming in the Pacific Ocean.

Lizzie shifted her feet again, reset her grip on the sack. Where had those boys gone, anyway? For that matter, where had all the jackrabbits gone? She certainly didn't see any running into her outstretched bag.

She was just preparing to stand up to stretch and see if she could locate her brothers' towheads above the swaying grass when a strange hooting, warbling sound sent a frisson of fear up her spine. "Wa-wa-wa-wah!"

Indians? Hadn't the men been talking, just last night, about how surprising it was that they hadn't seen any of the red savages before now?

Lizzie wanted to run, but she didn't know which way to go. In the direction her brothers had gone or back to camp? Going toward camp seemed better, except for the fact that the sound seemed to be coming from that way!

There was no point in worrying about which direction to run, though, because her muscles seemed to have locked, leaving her no choice but to go on crouching in the ravine, her bare feet rooted to the earth, her hands gripping the sack so tightly that her knuckles shone with a pale light.

"Wa-wa-wa-wa-wah!" she heard again. Growing closer this time. "Wa-wa-wa-wa-wah!" Whatever . . . *who*ever made the sound was clearly moving toward her, stopping, moving again. The hair on the back of her neck actually rose and stood stiff and straight.

Finally, beginning to get control of her muscles again, Lizzie turned, slowly, cautiously, toward the invading sound. Then she rose, clutching the burlap sack to her breast. If she could only see—

But then she *could* see. She could see every emigrant's worst nightmare come true in the bright light of day. At the edge of the small ravine, not ten feet away, an Indian man sat on a painted pony. He wore moccasins, a breech cloth, and leggings, tied below the knee by bands of beadwork, but no shirt at all, and his hair fell in two long, dark braids. He looked, in fact, exactly like what Lizzie had been taught to expect . . . a savage! But even as she stared at him, the "Wa–wa–wa–wah!" came again from the ravine. Closer this time.

The man didn't even glance back over his shoulder to see about the noise, so he must know. Those were more red savages, of course. Coming to attack her!

Still . . . the man on the pony didn't look ready to attack. In fact, he sat lightly on his horse, completely relaxed as far as Lizzie could tell, ignoring the approaching noise. He pointed to the burlap sack in her hands and indicated by a motion so delicate that Lizzie couldn't have said how she knew that he meant he wanted to know what she was doing with it. Apparently he had been watching her crouched there in the ravine, holding it open.

"Rabbits," she said, her voice quavering. "I'm catching rabbits." And in case he didn't understand English, she held her trembling hands up on each side of her head to indicate long ears.

The man nodded, putting his own hands along each side of his head to acknowledge her gesture. As he did so, a smile seemed to tweak at the corners of his mouth. But it couldn't have been a smile. Everyone said these savages never smiled, never laughed. All the emigrants knew that.

"My brothers," Lizzie added, pointing up the ravine in the direction away from the sound, which seemed to have stalled briefly in its approach. "My brothers are going to make the rabbits run into my sack." And she held the empty sack open and thrust a hand into it in imitation of a rabbit's blind flight into her trap.

The Indian gave no indication whether he understood her or

not. She hoped he had understood. Perhaps he would think her brothers were grown men, grown men with guns, and he and his shrieking companions would leave.

But just as she was searching the man's dark eyes, trying to decide whether he understood her, and of even more importance, what he was going to do next, two shouting, warbling creatures sprang at her out of the grass. They sprang, but then stopped, almost in midair.

It was John and Robert. Only John and Robert!

Lizzie's knees buckled, and she sat, suddenly and unexpectedly, on the ground.

The twins had been coming on so fast that they passed the man sitting quietly above Lizzie on horseback without seeming to see him. When they landed, though, they couldn't help but see, and they stopped, stock still, almost at the feet of the painted pony, their heads tipped back to stare. They stood so close to Lizzie that she could have reached out to slap them, one after the other. But she did not. It was more interesting to observe them, their mouths hanging open, their eyes practically bugged out of their heads.

So . . . the twins had brought her out here to play a trick on her. Nothing more. The realization flashed inside Lizzie, hard and bright. They had meant to frighten her by circling back and pretending to be savages on the warpath.

After only a few brief seconds of staring, Lizzie's older brothers showed their true mettle. With one loud "Whoop!" they leapt back up the ravine, heading toward camp, leaving the sister they'd been told to protect in their dust. The Indian man, the "savage," tipped his head back and laughed and laughed.

When he was through laughing, he turned his gaze once

more upon Lizzie. A softness, very like a smile, lingered about his mouth. She smiled back, tentatively, and rose to her feet again. She took a step in the direction of her brothers' escape.

But no, the man held up a hand to stop her. She didn't know whether she should honor his silent command or not, but there was something in his face—something that put her in mind, not of Papa, but of Mama when she had made up her mind and wouldn't be swayed—that caused Lizzie to obey.

The man reached to his belt and took down something she hadn't noticed before. One, two . . . no, three jackrabbits. So recently killed that they came limp and warm into her hands.

"Thank you," she said, bowing her head in her benefactor's direction. "Thank you very much." But the man and his pony were already moving away, and as they did, the sound of laughter floated, once more, on the prairie wind.

Lizzie took a deep breath. Then another. The second breath more steady than the first. So . . . her brothers' trick had worked. They had frightened her. She couldn't pretend otherwise. But maybe, after all, being afraid wasn't the worst thing. She hadn't run away, had she? Like Mama, she was still here.

Lizzie put the rabbits—one, two, three—into the sack her brothers had given her and, smiling, headed back toward camp.

The Boys in the Bushes

by Sonya Sones

Every day
on the way home from school
as we pass through the gate,

all the boys in our class
who have crushes on us
lie in wait.

Then they suddenly
leap from the bushes
and give us a bop.

And the strangest part is
that I feel kind of sad
when they stop.

And another weird thing:
if a boy likes me best,
he usually hits me much harder than all of the rest.

I sure wish
that someone would try
to help me understand why.

The Palazzo Funeral Parlor

by Marthe Jocelyn

I realized it the first minute we moved to apartment 2B at 233 Water Street. The taxi pulled up behind a hearse, outside our new front door. My mother paid the driver, and my little sister Lou scrambled out over my legs trying to be first. I looked up and saw right off that we'd be living on top of the Palazzo Funeral Parlor.

Maybe seven men were hanging around on the sidewalk, all wearing black suits and looking like gangsters with pointy black shoes and black hats. I guessed they were waiting to carry the coffin.

"You forgot to mention the added attraction, Mom," I said.

"What's that?" She pretended not to get my meaning.

I jerked my thumb toward the welcoming committee.

"It's a plus," said my mother. "The location keeps the price down, and there'll be no one to complain about the almighty racket of growing children."

But once it was in my head, I couldn't get it out. Dead bodies would be living downstairs.

• • •

The Sunday after we moved in I went to sit on the stoop, thinking I'd get acquainted with the neighborhood. We'd been so busy with boxes I hadn't had a chance to admit that I lived here yet, fourteen blocks away from our old place.

It's not like my life was going to be so different. I was still going to Glen Ames Middle School, only now I was far enough away to take the bus instead of walk, and I'd have to take Lou with me. She goes to Glen Ames Elementary. I'd still be taking piano lessons on Thursdays after school from Mrs. Wendicott and I'd still be delivering groceries on Saturday mornings for Two-Ton Carl at the Zippy Market on the corner of my old block. So it wasn't like my life was over or anything. It wasn't, like, next stop: Palazzo's.

The door behind me swung open and hit my back.

"Move," said Lou. Her name is Louisa, but I call her Lou. Or sometimes Flu if she's bothering me. She squeezed through the door as I shifted a step lower. She plopped herself down next to me and pulled out a pack of bubble gum.

"One, Rosie," she said. "You get exactly one."

She stretches her candy allowance for the whole week. Mine is gone by Saturday afternoon. We started our bubbles at the same second and mine was bigger by an inch at least. We sucked them in and started over.

A man came out of the heavy glass Palazzo doors and stood there looking up and down the street. He had a stubbly chin and a tomato face with not quite enough hair to stretch across the top. He took a couple of puffs from his cigarette while he eyed us and then flicked the butt onto the road where it lay smoking.

"That is so wrong," said Lou. She got up, like I knew she would, and went to stomp on that butt till it was tobacco dust.

Then she sat back down with her arms crossed on her chest like a ticked-off teacher. The bald guy just shook his head and went into Palazzo's.

"Have you told anybody where we live?" asked Lou.

"What do you mean?" I said.

"In a funeral parlor."

"We don't live IN the funeral parlor, Lou."

"Don't you want to look inside?" she asked.

"Why would I?"

"To see a body."

"Lou!"

"Before it gets chopped up."

"Lou!"

"Well? Aren't you curious?"

I had done everything I possibly could not to be curious, and here was Lou making me think about it.

"What are you saying, Lou? Is that the guy who chops up the bodies?"

"No way," said Lou. "He takes out the garbage and sweeps up. His fingers are too fat. I think it's his wife."

Wow, she'd thought about it already.

"I saw his wife in the laundry room," she said. "Mrs. Palazzo."

"That's not her name."

"I know that," said Lou. "She has extra white hands. From washing them in bleach after touching the bodies."

"I don't think a woman would have that job," I said. What I meant was, I wouldn't touch a dead body for a thousand dollars. "You think a cute little girl would say, 'Oh, I hope I'll grow up to work in a funeral parlor someday'?"

"You think a cute little boy would?"

Okay, so I didn't have the answer.

I mostly tried not to think about it after that.

A couple of weeks went by and then Mrs. Wendicott died.

Mrs. Wendicott was my piano teacher. I didn't see her die because she did it on a Monday, not on a Thursday between 3:30 and 4:00.

I was doing my history worksheet in the fat chair by the window, eating a grilled cheese sandwich. Lou was repeating her times tables so she could get a rainbow beside her name on the board the next day.

I saw the car roll up and watched while they carried Mrs. Wendicott into Palazzo's, only I didn't realize it was her because she was under a rubbery blanket, covered right up. But then I saw her son, Mr. Wendicott.

"Lou," I said. "Look at this."

"Eight times eight is sixty-four."

"No, I mean it. Shut up and come here."

"Eight times nine is seventy-two. Another corpse?"

"I think it's Mrs. Wendicott."

Even though it's not so nice to say, part of me was kind of relieved. Maybe I wouldn't have to take piano lessons anymore.

"Wow," said Lou. "Someone we know?"

They had disappeared from out front.

Lou inspected the floorboards. "What do you think they do first down there? Where exactly do they put her?"

"Aw, Lou! Why'd you have to ask that?" Now I'd be thinking about it. Does Mrs. Palazzo chop up the bodies under our kitchen? Or under my bedroom?

"I'm only wondering," said Lou.

"Wonder something else. Think up something pleasant about Mrs. Wendicott. That's what you're supposed to do."

I had some memories of Mrs. Wendicott, and they weren't all bad. Apart from making me sit there doing something I didn't want to be doing, she was a nice old lady.

She would say the same thing every time I knocked on her door.

"Well, now, Rosemarie. Are we ready to make music together?"

She'd sit next to me in her living room, with her bottom spilling over the edges of the piano bench. Her hands, covered in brown spots, rested on her lap. I could see her fingers twitch whenever I made a mistake, like she was longing to play the song herself.

There was a dish of peppermints, white-and-red-striped swirls, sitting on top of the piano. Mrs. Wendicott's breath came out in small, minty puffs, and sometimes she hummed along while I played.

She had three dresses, one green, one brown, and one like dark red wine. They were made of slinky, velvety material that draped over itself, the way the skin on her arms lay in silky folds when she was listening to the lesson. She had a brooch that she moved from collar to collar. It looked like a sunflower made out of a hundred tiny pearls. She always wore that pin, whichever dress she had on.

The lesson would end when Lou knocked on the door and it was her turn. Mrs. Wendicott would reach up for the peppermints and hold the bowl out to me like she was grateful that I'd spent half an hour with her and this was my reward. I'd wait in the kitchen while Lou played way better than me and then we walked home together.

When Mom got in from work, I put out plates for the take-out Mexican she brought.

"I hope you didn't buy the Blue Level piano book, Mom," I said. "I won't be needing it. I'm pretty sure Mrs. Wendicott is dead."

"What do you mean, Rosie?"

"She's downstairs," said Lou. "We saw the body bag."

"Oh, dear," said Mom. "Poor Mrs. Wendicott. I'll go down later and find out when they're having the visitation." She pried the tacos out of the aluminum dish and asked to hear Lou's times tables.

I started wondering what Mrs. Wendicott died of. Did she have a fit and fall over onto the piano keys, playing one last chord with her bosom? Or maybe she choked to death on a peppermint and lay there waving her freckled hands in the air, trying to catch a breath?

I didn't think I'd ask. It would be better if she just took a nap on the gold-striped sofa and died in a peaceful, old-lady way.

"Mom?" I asked. "Are they going to chop up Mrs. Wendicott's body?"

"No, sweetie. What gave you that idea? They'll actually spend some time fixing her up. Comb her hair in a pretty way. Put on her best dress for the funeral, stuff like that."

Mom thought she was making me feel better, but the truth is that what she said gave me the creeps. I didn't like the idea of a stranger's fingers playing around with Mrs. Wendicott's hair or choosing the brown dress over the dark red one, which I always preferred. And wait a minute! If the Palazzos were going to change her dress, they would see her underwear! For sure, she wouldn't like that.

I called my friend Tina.

"You're right, Rosie," she said after I explained. "The whole picture is kind of disturbing."

"Do you think I should write a letter to say that the red dress would be better?"

"It's not just a matter of the red dress, Rosie," said Tina, in her I-have-an-older-brother-and-therefore-the-most-information-on-any-given-topic voice. "My brother, Marco, says that dead bodies are subjected to numerous humiliations before they go to their final rest."

"What do you mean?"

"They get pumped full of chemicals and covered in makeup and junk like that. If the coffin is going to be open at the visitation."

"Open coffin?"

"Don't you know anything, Rosie? You live on top of a funeral parlor. You should be an expert by now!"

She was right. I should be the know-it-all on this topic. I was going to have to go into Palazzo's and do some investigating.

I lay in bed imagining I was playing First Etude very carefully, over and over, so I wouldn't be thinking about Mrs. Wendicott lying downstairs, pumped full of chemicals.

"This is our chance," Lou said to me on the bus home next day. "We can go tonight with Mom, to visit Mrs. Wendicott and scope out the place."

"Sure, why not?" I said. I wanted to throw up. But I was the big sister, after all. Lou might need me.

When we got off the bus, we could see Mr. Palazzo in the front hall of the funeral parlor, fumbling with a box of candles.

"Party time," said Lou.

Straight after homework, Mom started to mutter about what I was going to wear to Palazzo's, seeing as we don't usually go places where dressing up is necessary. I suggested clean blue jeans and she said no, I'd have to use one of her skirts rolled over at the top. Lou could make do with one of the dresses I'd outgrown without ever wearing.

By the time we got there, Mr. Palazzo was standing in the foyer, wearing a black suit, a shiny tie, and a nasty dose of cologne. The candles he'd been playing with earlier were lit, giving off a warm, holy feel.

Mr. Wendicott was at the next set of doors, shaking hands with everybody and murmuring, "Thank you, thank you," over and over. When it was our turn, Mom said, "We're so sorry about your loss, Mr. Wendicott. These are my girls, Rosemarie and Louisa. They were students of your mother's."

Mr. Wendicott shook my hand and said, "Thank you, thank you," even though I hadn't said anything. As we moved along, I felt sort of prickly with the itch of somebody else's suffering.

"Is there food here?" asked Lou.

I swatted her and dragged her into the big room, ready to check the layout of the place. I wanted to know if anything disgusting happened below where our bedroom was. The main area would have been under our living room and probably Mom's room, too. The walls were covered in something gray and nubbly, not regular paint. The windows had blue satiny shades pulled down.

About fifteen people were standing around, whispering as if they were in a library. Mrs. Palazzo was adjusting the cloth on a side table. She had smooth hair and squinty eyes and wore a navy suit to match her curtains. I made an extra effort not to look at her fingers.

Exactly together, the next second, was when Lou and I saw it. I mean, her. Mrs. Wendicott. My shoes felt like they were suddenly stuck to the floor with Krazy Glue.

The coffin was huge and white. The lid was open. And she was in there.

"Whoa," I said, putting out my hand to grab Lou's.

"Holy Moly," said Lou, squeezing me back.

My head got hot and foggy. Lou's nails were half an inch into my wrist before I noticed and shook free.

"Girls?" said my mother, right behind us.

"Ahh!" She scared me to bits.

"Have you had enough?" asked Mom. "I think it would be okay to go, now we've paid our respects."

"Mom!" I whispered. "That's her."

I jutted my chin toward the coffin.

"Oh," said my mother. "No wonder you're standing here like zombies. I don't blame you. I never liked an open coffin myself. Let's go home and have supper."

She guided us gently toward the exit and we almost got out, except Mrs. Palazzo tapped Mom's arm and asked if we wouldn't mind stepping into the office for a moment.

I was relieved to see that the office was under where my room is upstairs, and they'd fixed it up really nicely with glowing lampshades and soft cushions. No bodies, no blood.

Mrs. Palazzo slid in behind her desk and Mom sat in front of it, with Lou leaning on her. I sat in another chair, off to the side of the desk.

"I realize this is not the best time," Mrs. Palazzo was saying. Her voice is one of those extra quiet ones that force you to lean close. "But I never seem to see you during business hours."

She started to fiddle with some coins in a dish on her desk, clinking them, turning them over. My eyes went straight to her long, white fingers. I tried not to think about what kept them busy during business hours, but I was getting a picture of guts spilling like spaghetti out of Mrs. Wendicott.

"It's just that you've been leaving your recycling in the hallway," said Mrs. Palazzo, "and it needs to go into the disposal room to await the weekly pickup."

"Oh, I'm sorry," said Mom. "I didn't realize."

Mrs. Palazzo shook the dish, rattling the coins and some other bitty things I could see in there, too. A couple of keys, a ring, the cap to a pen.

"You go down the back stairs," she said, picking a key out of the dish. "It's the first door on your left and you'll need this. The room is connected to our clinic on the inside."

Mom stood up and took the key. The word *clinic* was ringing in my head while I stared at the dish. Mrs. Wendicott's brooch was sitting there, plain as day, surrounded by nickels and dimes. The pearl sunflower. I would have recognized it anywhere.

"Thank you," said Mom, moving to go. "That will be a good chore for the girls." Mrs. Palazzo laughed, more of a wheeze, and got ahead of my mother to open the door.

I widened my eyes at Lou, getting her to follow the jerk of my head. She saw the brooch and swept her hand out to snatch it in less than a second. She's a wonder, that Lou. She knelt down to fuss with her shoelace and stuffed the brooch into her sock, smooth as on TV. I couldn't believe it. We fumbled our way past Mrs. Palazzo, leaving Mom kind of bemused while we ran upstairs.

We dove onto Lou's bed. I was dizzy.

"This is so wrong," said Lou, not meaning her own act of daredevil thievery. "Those Palazzos are grave robbers."

"She should be wearing her brooch," I agreed. "She never took it off."

"You think she wore it on her jammies?"

"You think she wore jammies? I bet she wore one of those nightie things that grannies wear in storybooks."

"The funeral is tomorrow," said Lou. "She's still down there. You know what we should do?"

I wished I didn't, but I did.

We were perfect daughters all evening. We made scrambled eggs and toast for supper, with hot chocolate. We cleaned up after and we offered to take the recycling to its new destination. This was part of the plan, of course. The "disposal room" was our only hope for access to the funeral parlor.

"Don't lose the key," said Mom. "I have a feeling our landlady would not be happy."

The disposal room should have been named the Stink Closet. There was a blue bin for cans and bottles, a blue box for newspapers, and a wide chute from Palazzo's leading directly into a big, smelly garbage container. The obvious solution was so disgusting neither of us could say it out loud.

We went back upstairs to prepare. We both put on two pairs

of jammies for protection. I put my ugly ones on the outside. We got the rubber gloves from under the sink so we'd each have one clean hand anyway. Hats. Flashlights. Disposal room key. Apartment key. Brooch. We were ready. We brushed our teeth and pretended to go to bed. Mom went to bed. It was so easy this far, it didn't seem real.

The Stink Closet made it real. When we got in there it was pitch black, and we had to shift the jumbo garbage can out of the way.

"I never knew anything could smell this bad," said Lou.

"We should have brought nose-plugs," I said.

"Do you think they toss the guts through here?" asked Lou.

"No way," I said, pretty sure it was true. "They have special sanitary receptacles for stuff like that. This is just regular rotten garbage."

I thought Lou should go through the chute first because she's always first. She figured it should be me. As usual, she won.

"It's a bit gunky," she whispered, holding the flap up. "My rubber glove is sticking."

"Oh, thanks," I said, tugging my hat on low. I turned my head sideways and reached into the chute. It was only a couple of feet to the other end. I pulled myself through, trying not to think of all the slime that had made the trip before me. Lou came right behind me, no trouble at all, and there we were in the clinic, with white counters and metal tables glowing faintly in the dark.

"I don't like this," said Lou, shivering.

"No talking," I whispered.

We pushed through the door into their big reception area.

The coffin was in the same place, only shut now. A couple of lamps had been left on, so there was soft, yellow light on everything. The flowers smelled too sweet.

"Where do you think the Palazzos sleep?" asked Lou, looking around. I'd been wondering so hard about where the dead person was sleeping, I hadn't thought about where the living ones might be.

"I bet he snores," said Lou. "With his hair flopping off his head like half a wig."

"Lou. Shut up."

In order to accomplish our mission, someone would have to open the coffin. Lou just stood there, shaking her head.

I pulled off my rubber glove and clenched my fists. I took three giant steps forward. I held my breath the way you're supposed to when you drive past a cemetery, in case the ghosts fly in. I grabbed the polished handle and flung up the lid.

I was face to face with Mrs. Wendicott.

I was happy to see she was wearing the wine red dress. Then I noticed that Tina's brother was right about the makeup. She was slathered. The skin-colored stuff and lots of blush plus purply eye shadow, which she never would have worn. Her hair was in fancy waves, like she'd spent the afternoon at Evelyn's Snip'n'Curl. She looked like she couldn't quite make it till midnight at a New Year's Eve party and had to take a quick nap.

"Hi, Mrs. Wendicott," I said, real quiet. "We're here to give you something you might be missing." I felt Lou take a step closer behind me and her fingers slipped the brooch into my hand.

I didn't know I was trembling till I tried to clip the pin part on the sunflower. What if I stabbed her? Would blood come out or chemicals? But the pin slid easily through the silky red fabric below the collar, right where she always wore it. Then I fumbled again. I couldn't get the clasp fastened.

"Leave it," Lou whispered. "It's not like she's going to shake it off."

Lou was standing next to me now, holding my arm. Closing the lid again seemed sort of rude.

"Let's say a blessing first," I said.

"What should we say?"

I licked my lips and took a breath. "Dear Mrs. Wendicott. Thank you for teaching us and for making music. We hope your song plays forever in our hearts. Good-bye. Sincerely, Rosemarie."

"And Louisa," said Lou. "That was more like a letter," she added to me. "But it was nice."

"Thanks," I said. I pulled the lid down as gently as I could, and we hightailed it out of there, by the same way we had come in.

Later, in our beds, we replayed the night.

"You were brave," said Lou. "I don't think I could have done that. Touched her."

"Somehow it wasn't so hard," I said, "knowing I was doing the right thing."

Mom was more than amazed when I put in a load of laundry before breakfast.

"I'm out of jammies," I told her. "No big deal."

"I ran into our landlady this morning when I went out for

milk," said Mom. "They had a break-in last night at the funeral parlor."

Lou stopped chewing her Eggo. My heart stopped beating.

"They did?" I never heard my own voice squeak before.

"Did they call the cops?" asked Lou.

Mom kept spreading peanut butter on our lunch sandwiches.

"The thief left behind a pair of gloves," she said. "But there only seems to be one thing missing, so they might not bother with the police. It was a piece of jewelry they were holding for Mrs. Wendicott's son."

Lou's shoe whacked my shin under the table. My face felt so hot, it would have burned toast.

"The jewelry wasn't valuable," said Mom, not noticing us. "Her son doesn't care, apparently. It was just a trinket Mrs. Wendicott's husband gave her on their honeymoon. Nothing worth stealing."

I stared into Lou's eyes.

"We'll be late for the bus!" she yelled, and we kicked up such a rumpus getting out the door that Mom forgot what she was saying.

"We didn't really steal it, did we?" asked Lou, on the Number 12 bus.

"WE didn't," I said. "YOU did." I was remembering how quick she'd been.

"But—"

I cut off her protest. "That's not the point. Mrs. Palazzo didn't steal it either. She was saving it for the son."

"But Mrs. Wendicott loved that brooch," said Lou. "Her husband gave it to her."

"Yeah," I said. "She wore it every day of her life. We just made it so now she'll wear it every day of her death, too."

"Will her body wear it or her ghost?" asked Lou. "Because her body is going to rot."

"Her ghost," I said. "Her ghost will wear the brooch and her ghost husband will see she still has it and they'll live happily ever after. Thanks to us. The end."

Bird

by Margaret Peterson Haddix

We still lived on the farm the summer I was twelve. When we were younger, my brother and I had considered the whole place our playground. We spent hours playing hide-and-seek in the corn, chasing baby pigs in the lot, climbing trees in the woods.

But that summer, I had other things on my mind. I worried that Mary Lynn Dobbins' mom would let her shave her legs and wear hose before my mother would let me and that my straight, limp, dirt-colored hair would never look like anything but straight, limp, dirt-colored hair. And even if I wanted to play—even if Mom gave me a moment's break from canning, cleaning, hoeing, and all the other work—even then, my brother was too busy helping my dad and playing football to care anymore about little-kid games.

My brother was going to try out for the high school team in the fall, and that scared me somehow. Bill was just two years older than me. When he'd come home from practice with the shoulder pads slung around his neck, I had to squint real hard to make my eyes see him as someone I knew.

Bill had already left for practice one night when the phone rang during supper.

"Cattle must be out again," Dad said, sighing, as Mom went to answer it.

"Maybe it's something else," I suggested without much hope. Most of our phone calls lately had brought bad news. Twice in the past week Dad and Bill had had to trample through neighbors' fields trying to find and retrieve lost cows, then spend a hot day repairing fallen fence posts and barbed wire. I knew as well as Dad did that he needed to replace the whole fence. But that would cost too much.

Dad slumped over his plate. For the first time I noticed lines around his gray eyes. His hair was normally the same color as mine, but tonight it was lightened several shades by hay dust he hadn't bothered to wash out. He and Bill had been baling all day, working frantically to finish before some predicted storm. The rain hadn't come, but they stumbled into the house so exhausted that Mom fussed about Dad getting sick and Bill needing to skip practice, just this once. Neither listened to her.

"Dad—it will be okay, won't it?" I asked.

"What?" He hadn't even heard me.

But I wasn't sure exactly what I had meant, and I'd lost the nerve to ask again.

"Nothing," I said.

Mom came back to the table.

"Where are they?" Dad asked wearily. "Which neighbor was that, complaining?"

"What?" Mom was startled. Her cheeks were flushed, and she was even grinning a little. "Oh, that wasn't about the cattle. Remember Ellen Hutchell? She's coming to visit."

Even I recognized the name. Ellen had been my mother's best friend all through school. And then, in some amazing turn of events, Ellen had met and fallen in love with a fabulously wealthy doctor—a heart specialist—and moved to California. As far as I knew, she hadn't come back to Indiana since. Every Christmas, she had her parents flown out to California for a visit.

"Why now?" Dad asked.

"She said she wants to make sure her kids know what pigs look like," Mom said. "*I* think she's homesick."

"Who wouldn't be?" Dad said. He raised his eyes toward the window at the end of the table. The last glow of sunset reflected off the roof of the barn. A blanket of shadows had fallen over the even rows of corn and the sleeping pigs. For a second, I felt like Dad had answered the question I hadn't dared repeat. Yes, everything would be okay. Of course it would.

Mom snapped the end from a peapod, slid a fingernail along its spine, and flicked the peas into the pot she balanced between her knees. I took another pod and did the same, though not as quickly. The peas echoed as they hit the bottom of my pan.

"I bet Mrs. Hutchell would let me wear hose and high heels if I were her daughter," I said.

"Probably, but you're my daughter, not hers," Mom said calmly. Then she laughed. "When we were kids, Ellen saved her money for months and sneaked into town to buy some bright red shoes with heels that must have been four inches high. She brought them in a bag to church—to church, can you believe it?—and changed in the bathroom. We were all in Sunday school and heard her coming way down the hall, clomping like a horse."

"Was she the first person in your class to get them? How old was she then?" I pushed a line of peas too hard, and three flew over the rim of my pot. They bounced across the porch and down the steps, coming to rest against curls of peeling paint.

"Pick them up. They'll all have to be washed, anyway," Mom said. She waited, frowning, then answered my questions.

"Ellen got those shoes before the rest of us had even thought about growing up," Mom said. "We were jealous until we saw how mad her parents were. I think her dad took her home and spanked her right then. She was so embarrassed. I mean, at her age—we were at least fourteen."

"That old? That's too young for high heels?" My heart sank. The three peas made a forlorn *plink* when I dropped them in my pan.

"We'll have to wait and see," Mom said.

I looked off at the heat shimmering above the cornfield. Everything was so still I felt like time had stopped. Bill would always be half-grown-up; Mary Lynn would always be ahead of me. I would always be waiting.

Distantly I heard the phone ring inside the house.

"Want to get that?" Mom said.

I put my pan down, pushed in through the screen door, and picked up the phone.

Mary Lynn's voice rushed at me through the receiver.

"Anything new in your boring life?" she asked. I heard the familiar *pop!* that meant she was chewing gum.

"Yes, there is," I shot back. "Mom's best friend from high school is coming to visit. She lives in California and has a little girl and two boys who are teenagers—"

"Are they cute?"

I knew she meant the boys, not the little girl.

"I don't know," I admitted.

"What's wrong with you, Jeanie? Can't you find out the important stuff?"

"I just haven't asked yet. Mary Lynn, I can't talk very long because Mom wants me to—"

"I know, I know. You're the slave. Call me back if you can come over this afternoon."

"Okay."

But I wasn't sure I would. If I went over to Mary Lynn's, we'd spend all afternoon playing with her sister's curling iron—Mary Lynn's long blond hair curled perfectly—and using her mother's makeup, if her mother wasn't around. Then Mary Lynn would brag about how she was going to get her own curling iron and makeup when she turned thirteen in the fall. It wasn't fair.

Mom had finished shelling peas when I got back to the porch, but she was sitting still, not gathering up the pods to throw to the pigs.

"Mary Lynn?" she asked.

I nodded. She squinted at something beyond the cornfield, maybe the Comstocks' barns or even the clock tower of the county courthouse five miles away.

"You know, Mary Lynn's a lot like Ellen was, growing up—always trying to set the rules for the rest of us to follow. But you don't have to follow."

I just stared at my right tennis shoe, where my little toe poked through the ragged canvas. Mom began clearing the mess from the peas.

"Bill and your dad will be in to eat soon. Why don't you go on in and get the ham started?"

. . .

I wedged one bare foot between two branches, feeling the rough bark cut into my skin. I shoved maple leaves out of the way. Another limb higher, I found the perch that let me see miles up the road.

It was August 13, the date that had been circled on our Reynolds Fertilizer Co. calendar for a month. Every morning when I wrote the day's hog prices on the calendar for my dad, I had looked at that red circle and the words inside: "Ellen— 3 P.M."

My watch said it was five minutes after three now, but there was no movement on the gravel road, not even a pickup or a tractor.

In a month of shelling peas and hoeing and canning corn with Mom, I'd found out everything. Ellen had met her doctor when she went to work as a secretary in Cincinnati. He saw her on the street and was bewitched right away—at least that was what Ellen had told Mom. They eloped to California two months later.

"I thought it was so romantic then," Mom had said, then tightened her lips in a way I didn't understand.

I wanted to meet the doctor, to see someone that romantic myself. I thought it was perfect that he was a heart specialist. But he wasn't coming, just Ellen and the kids. The boys were sixteen and fourteen and the little girl was five. When I asked what they looked like, Mom had dug out a picture from last year's Christmas card, and I'd smuggled it over to Mary Lynn's. She said the boys were incredible; they looked just like the guys in the prom issue of *Seventeen*. One of the boys had dark hair that waved back just right; and the other, the younger one, had red-brown hair that touched the edge of his collar. Both had wide blue eyes and perfect tan faces. Their names were Derek and Evan, and Mary Lynn said that was perfect, too, like soap opera names. Mary Lynn watched soap operas all the time. My mom wouldn't let me.

Mary Lynn didn't pay any attention at all to the little girl, except to make fun of her name. It was Marisol, but Mary Lynn kept pretending to forget. *"Parasol?"* she'd say mockingly. "Who'd name their kid after an umbrella?" That bothered me, but I didn't say so. In the picture beside her muscular brothers, Marisol looked tiny and blond, like a porcelain doll.

Now I stared up the road. Still no sign of the Hutchells. I peered down at the roof of our house, counted the brown spots where shingles had fallen off. From my perch in the tree the house look small, just an *L*-shaped box with a tiny porch in the crook of the *L*. What would the Hutchells think of it? What would they think of me?

Out of the corner of my eye, I saw a stirring of dust far up the road. It was them—and I was still in the tree. What would they think of that? I half-slid, half-climbed down the trunk, scraping my knees and banging my ankles. When I reached the second-to-last branch, I jumped, hitting the ground so hard I fell over onto a hard, exposed root.

"Jeanie, what's wrong?" Mom asked as I rushed into the house. She was taking a tray of chocolate hazelnut cookies out of the oven. I'd shelled the nuts myself.

"They're almost here," I said, and ran up to my room to comb my hair and pull on my new white tennis shoes, bought the week before for me to wear back to school.

I sat down on my bed and heard my mother opening the front door.

"Ellen!—and this must be Derek and Evan and Marisol."

"Well, Carol, it's been a long time, hasn't it?" a husky voice replied. "Come on, kids. Say hello."

I heard mumblings, then Ellen continued, "And where are your two?"

"Bill's outside working with Jim, but they should be in soon. They were watching for you. Jeanie's around here somewhere—Jeanie?" Mom called.

I realized that I had balled both hands into fists, clutching the flowered bedspread. Slowly I let go and pushed myself up. In my dresser mirror, my eyes were wide and scared-looking. If only I could wear makeup—

"Jeanie?" Mom called again. I walked out of my room and down the stairs.

Derek and Evan were leaning on the couch, the bright colors of their shirts and shorts making it look even more faded. Mary Lynn would have died to see them: They were even better-looking in person, with tans and wind-blown hair. They looked bored already.

I didn't see the little girl at first. She was half-hidden behind her mother, clutching onto Mrs. Hutchell's pants and sucking her thumb.

Mrs. Hutchell ignored her and stretched out her arms to me. She drew me into a hug. I smelled cigarette smoke and a spicy perfume in her silky blouse, and then she released me.

"You are the spitting image of Carol at your age," she said. "I feel like I'm a kid again, just looking at you."

"That was a long time ago, wasn't it?" Mom laughed.

"Don't remind me!" Mrs. Hutchell said, shaking her head.

"Boys, don't Carol and I look like a pair of teenagers even now?"

Derek shrugged; Evan didn't move. Really, in spite of her fancy clothes and high heels, Mrs. Hutchell looked even older than Mom. Her hair was teased and sprayed, just so, and her skin was stretched tight across her face, but her eyes were hard. I might have even said they looked sad, but what did she have to be sad about?

"Oh, let me get you something to drink," Mom said. "Lemonade? Iced tea? Coke? Milk?"

"Just some mineral water for me," Mrs. Hutchell said.

"It'll have to be well water, if that's okay," Mom said.

"Sure," Mrs. Hutchell said. "That's fine." She turned to her boys again. "See, kids, out here, their water comes straight from the ground. It's not what you're used to, is it?"

I thought I saw Evan roll his eyes. I burned with shame as I helped Mom get the drinks and bring out the cookies. Why hadn't Mom known Mrs. Hutchell would want mineral water—whatever that was?

Bill and Dad arrived just as everyone started eating, and Mrs. Hutchell had to rave about how tall Bill was.

Bill ignored her and turned to Derek.

"You play football?" he asked.

"First string," he said. "Evan plays, too."

I scrunched back against the wall, wishing I'd thought of something—anything—to say to them.

"Want to play now?" Bill was asking.

"Sure."

Mrs. Hutchell stopped them.

"You can play football in California. Why don't you have Bill and Jeanie show you around the barn and the rest of the farm?" She bent down and gave Marisol a little push. "You go, too, Marisol. Wouldn't you like to see a cuddly little pig?"

I was thinking that Mrs. Hutchell had forgotten a lot about farms, herself, if she thought pigs were cuddly. I was relieved when Marisol silently shook her head and clutched her mother again. Mary Lynn's jokes didn't seem so outlandish now—the little girl did seem about as frilly and decorative and useless as a parasol. With her doll-like curls and lacy dress, I just couldn't see taking her anywhere near manure.

The boys, at least, were edging toward the door. I started to follow.

"Jean Elizabeth, you are not wearing your good shoes out to the barn!" Mom declared.

Mortified, I went back to my room to change into my old holey ones. It would be better just to hide here, I thought. But I went back down through the living room and out the door, being careful not to glance toward the grown-ups. I had to run to catch up with the boys.

They were still talking football, but Evan actually glanced at me.

"Parents are awful, aren't they?" he said.

"Yeah." I grinned at him, feeling good. But I couldn't think of anything else to say.

Derek overheard.

"Parents stink," he said. "You know what Mom makes us do? She doesn't want Grandma and Grandpa to know that her and Dad are divorced, so she's making us lie to them. We're going to be there for a week, and we have to lie every day."

"They're divorced?" I asked, remembering the romantic doctor, the elopement to California. I stumbled on a dry tuft of grass.

"Yeah, they hated each other for years, but Mom always pretended. I bet she hasn't even told your mom," Evan said.

"I don't think my mom lies to your mom," I said.

Bill glared at me like I'd said something dumb.

Derek laughed.

"And Mom tells us everything, because she doesn't have anyone to talk to since Dad left. I bet we know things you don't know."

"Like what?" Bill asked.

"Like—your dad's going to lose the farm if he doesn't make a big—what's it called?—mortgage payment in September. And there's no way he's going to be able to make it, so you guys are going to move to town and he's going to get a job at some dog food factory."

"What? That's not true!" I said. I had to stop walking for a minute before I could trust my legs. I stared at the barn in front of us and then back to the house I had always lived in. It couldn't be true. I thought of Dad's face the night of the phone call and nearly cried. I looked over at Bill for help.

His face might as well have been carved of stone.

"Oh, well," he said. "The school in town has a better football team."

We reached the barn, and I looked at every pig and cow as if it were the last time I'd see one. Trailing the boys, I moved stiffly out to the barnyard and leaned against the fence, dangling foxtails over the edge for the pigs to sniff.

"They stink," Derek said, wrinkling his nose. "If I was you, I'd be glad to move."

One of the barn cats, an orange calico, darted through the pigs' legs and pounced on a patch of dirt on the other side of the fence. She growled at something between her paws.

"What's that?" Evan asked.

"A bird, I think," Bill said.

We all circled the hog lot toward the cat. She'd trapped a baby pigeon that had evidently fallen out of its nest. The bird's head leaned weakly to the side, and it opened its mouth slowly three times, in silence. The fourth time a soft "—ee—" came out.

"That's the ugliest bird I've ever seen," Evan said.

Its skin was still transparent, showing bones and black veins. Only the beginnings of feathers edged the tips of the scrawny wings.

"Watch. She'll play with it before she eats it," Bill said. "That's what they do."

With one paw, the cat batted the bird's head down, again and again and again. Each time the pigeon feebly lifted its head, the cat hit again. Then the cat half-threw the bird straight out, free. The bird struggled to right itself, urgently flapping wings that weren't meant to fly yet. The cat pounced again.

"—ee—" the bird moaned.

"I didn't know cats were so mean," Derek said.

Bill picked up a stone and skipped it across the hard dirt toward the cat. The cat jumped out of the way, and the stone hit the bird. The bird slid helplessly into a clump of straw.

"Good shot!" Derek said. He grabbed a rock, too, and threw it. His hit a few feet up on the barn door. Bill picked up a handful of stones and gave some to Evan and some to Derek. The cat was pulling the bird from the straw when three stones hit it at once.

Bill laughed, crazily, and grabbed more stones.

I watched another round of stones hit the cat, the bird, the barn. Before I knew what I was doing, I ran in front of the stones. One hit me in the calf.

"Stop!" I yelled. "Just—stop!"

My voice slid into sobs, and tears blinded me so that I couldn't see the boys looking at me. With one hand I scooped up the cat and shoved her inside the barn. With the other I picked up the bird and ran.

I didn't know where I was going until I reached the tree I had climbed earlier. Tucking the bird into my shirt pocket, I climbed even higher than before. Finally I stopped and leaned against a limb, panting and sweating and sobbing. The world whirled around me, but I held the tree tight.

After a while, I saw the boys come out of the barnyard. Bill went into the house for his football. They kicked it back and forth in the cattle pasture, and I heard Evan and Derek complaining every now and then about stepping in manure. But Bill wouldn't let them stop.

I looked down and saw Mom and Dad and Mrs. Hutchell inside the front window. I couldn't see Marisol. But every once in a while Mrs. Hutchell would throw back her head and laugh. Mom and Dad looked happy, too. How could they?

I didn't think Mrs. Hutchell had told them about the divorce. And they weren't talking about losing the farm.

But suddenly I was sure it was all true. Mrs. Hutchell was divorced. We were going to lose the farm; we were going to move

into town. I gulped down more sobs and stared out at the cornfield across the road. The stalks were past full tassel now and
starting to turn brown. Heat shimmered in the distance, but
looking at it now I felt time advancing. We would lose the farm
and move to town. Bill would start high school and outgrow
me. Mary Lynn would get to wear makeup and heels and probably even start dating long before me. Everything would change,
but never the way I wanted it to.

"Hello?" someone called timidly from below.

It was the little girl. Marisol. I held my breath, as if that would
make her go away. But she'd seen me. She knew exactly where
I was.

"How'd you get up there?" she asked.

"Climbed," I said.

She was silent for a minute. Then she said, "I saw what you
did. Mom made me go outside so she could talk grown-up talk.
I saw the boys being mean, and throwing stones, and then you
saved the bird. . . . You were so brave."

Brave? Me?

I'd almost forgotten about the bird. I eased it out of my
pocket. Its beak and claw caught in my cotton shirt, and I
thought for a minute that it was trying to stay there. But then I
saw: It was dead, its head and wings permanently drooping.

"The bird died anyway," I said roughly. "I didn't save it at
all." The words caught in my throat the same way the bird's
beak had caught in my pocket.

"It would have been deader without you," the little girl said.

That didn't make sense. Still, I kind of knew what she meant.

I looked down at Marisol looking up at me. Her eyes were

wide and awestruck, like someone staring at a movie star or a hero. If your mother dressed you like an ornamental doll—if your parents had hated each other for years—if you were Marisol, maybe a girl in a tree would look like a hero.

"Hey," I said roughly. "Do you want to help me bury the bird?"

But Marisol shook her head.

"Not in the ground," she said. "Up there."

She pointed, and I thought at first that she meant the sky. Yeah, right, I almost said, let's dig a hole in the clouds. But she was really pointing at the tree, with its branches spread heavenward.

That was one smart little girl.

"Okay," I said. "But you have to help."

I climbed down and gave her a leg up. Even in the frilly dress, she wasn't a bad climber. We laid the bird in a hollow between two branches and covered its body with leaves.

My family moved to town in the fall, after harvest. Bill used his football muscles for carrying boxes; and Mom hung our old, familiar curtains over windows that looked out on the trailer next door, instead of cornfields. Dad paced in our tiny backyard, and I heard him and Mom reassuring each other, "Just for a while. Just until we're back on our feet. We can make do until then."

Bill said he'd seen the column of numbers in Dad's account book. Bill said we were never going to get back on our feet. He said we'd be making do forever. I'd always have to wear second-hand clothes that the other kids made fun of. I'd always have to eat paper-bag lunches while the other kids sneaked out to restaurants. I'd always have to come home to an empty house, because Mom and Bill had part-time jobs, too.

But that fall, while we were making do, I thought about the bird a lot. I thought about how Marisol and I had left its body, sheltered and safe. I thought about how Marisol believed I'd rescued it, believed I was a hero, believed I was brave. And somehow that made me brave, for real.

New World Dreams

by Elaine Marie Alphin

Katie Reilly stood on the rough plank dock, gazing at the Boston harbor in dismay. The New World was nothing like what Mama had promised.

When Katie was small, Mama used to sing her dreams to make Katie feel safe. After Da died in the mine last year, it became harder and harder to heat their cramped Dublin room and put food on their table. Mama said they had no future in Ireland. And she started singing her dreams again, even though Katie was much too old for lullabies.

Hush little daughter, don't you cry.
Mama's gonna sing you a lullaby.
And if our Dublin home's gone cold,
The New World's streets are paved with gold.

Maybe Mama hoped that the song would make them both feel safe. It would be a whole new land, Mama promised, not just the New World of the colonies. People in this new land talked about independence from the Old World. Mama said that meant new opportunities for everyone, including the Reilly family. All she and Katie had to do was find a way to get there.

"We're too poor to pay for the journey," Mama explained. "But there's always a way to make your dreams come true, Katie girl. They don't have enough workers for all the jobs that need doing in the New World."

The way Mama said "New World" it sounded like the Promised Land. Katie wasn't sure she believed in promises or dreams anymore, not since Da had died and things had just gotten worse and worse. But Mama had lost Da, too, and it hadn't made her stop believing. Somehow it had given her new determination to follow her dreams.

"If we bind ourselves by an indenture to an employer in the colonies," she explained, her lilting voice bright with hope, "why, then he'll pay our passage on the ship! And once we work for the time in the indenture, he'll give us good clothing and our own land. We can start over as free people in the New World."

New possibilities, Mama promised. New dangers, Katie thought.

Now she looked at the streets that stretched away from the dock. There were no golden pavements, only sodden mud, with wooden boards over the worst puddles. She wished they could get on the ship and sail back home, back to the old world where she didn't feel so strange and out of place.

"The Reilly women," a ship's officer called.

Katie slowly followed Mama into the muddy street, where the ship's officer was handing half of their indenture contract to a strange man. After Mama and Katie had signed the indenture, the ship's captain had torn it in half and given one piece to

Mama. He'd kept the other piece to turn over to their new employer.

The strange man looked at them, his thick brows drawn together in anger, and Katie looked right back at him, surprised at his outrage when she was the one who had reason to feel angry. The man complained, "I paid passage for two able-bodied servants in my contract. I don't want a child. I already have a baby daughter of my own."

Katie saw a young woman standing behind the man. Her fine skirts dragged in the mud, and she clutched a baby wrapped in a woolen blanket. The baby cried loudly, and the woman rocked it with nervous jerks.

Mama said, "My daughter can do her share of the work, Master Benton."

"She's only a child," he said. "You'll end up tending her instead of keeping my home. I must sell her contract to a larger family, to someone who can use an extra kitchen girl."

Katie gasped, but Mama spoke up in a firm voice. "No, Master Benton. If my Katie does not stay, I'll return to Ireland with her."

"Good," muttered Katie. The baby's thin, keening wail chilled her.

"You cannot leave," Master Benton told Mama sharply. He held up his torn portion of the contract. "By the terms of your indenture, you must work as you promised or repay your passage money. But the child must go."

Now Mama looked worried. Katie knew they had no money to repay their passage. "I would work to repay you, sir," Mama stammered.

Could this man really send her to a strange family without

Mama? Katie felt tears burning behind her eyelids and fought to keep them from falling. The effort gave her a sick, empty feeling inside, the way she had felt when the mine tolled its bell to warn people about the cave-in where Da had died. Katie couldn't bear to lose Mama as she had lost Da! But how could she explain that to Master Benton, with his hard, unsympathetic face?

The baby cried in shrill, choking gasps, and the young mother whispered to it and squeezed the blanket more tightly around it. This must be her first, Katie thought—she has no idea how to quiet the child. And that gave Katie courage, because she'd spent many hours minding neighbor babies back in Dublin. She took a deep breath. "I know how to quiet your baby," she told the woman. "Please let me try."

"Keep silent, child," Master Benton snapped.

The woman patted the screaming baby helplessly. Then she tried rocking it with no success.

"My daughter can help," said Mama. "Just give her a chance." Her voice sounded desperate.

The baby stopped screaming, and the woman breathed a sigh of relief. Then it took a deep breath and started again.

Katie went to the young woman and stretched out her arms. "Please, Mistress, may I hold the baby?"

The woman looked exhausted and as close to tears as Katie felt herself. "Try, child," she said.

Katie cradled the baby girl and sang a bit of Mama's song. *"Hush little daughter . . ."*

The baby choked out a few last sobs, then sighed, and the woman's eyes grew large. Katie tickled the tiny fingers and the little girl giggled. It might not be so bad to have a baby sister.

Then she reminded herself that the baby would never be part of her family for real, even if the man agreed to let her stay.

"See?" Mama told him. "My daughter can be of use."

"Please," Katie said, hating the begging sound in her voice. But she couldn't bear being sent away to yet another new place, this time with no family at all. "Please, Master Benton, I can help."

The man looked at the quiet baby and then at his smiling wife. His angry face softened. Finally he said, "The girl may stay on trial."

Katie helped Mama drag the hall rug into the yard so they could beat the dust out of it. "Thank you, Katie girl," Mama said, smiling. "It's been a whole month and Master hasn't sent you away. I think all will be well for us here."

Katie knew that Mama wanted her to agree. And in the past month she had grown fond of the baby, Sarah, and even learned her way around Boston. She was coming to like this rough, new country where people smiled instead of ignoring her because she was somebody's servant. Back in Ireland, folk looked down on other people's servants.

"I love taking care of baby Sarah," she admitted finally, "but we work all the time. And Master Benton still does not care for me."

"He's seen how hard you work," Mama said quickly. "I think he is content. And we're together." Mama beat the rugs with vigor. "'Tis a bigger house than our room in Dublin, too, and warmer with the rugs on the floors."

Katie sighed and pointed out, "A bigger house means it takes longer to clean the floors and beat the rugs and scrub the clothes and wash the dishes—"

Mama laughed. "You should make that into your own song."

"Can I just make up a song, the way you do?" asked Katie. The idea surprised her.

"Of course you can," said Mama. "If the want is in you, the song will come."

Katie sang,

Weed the garden and stir the stew,
Rock the baby, there's more to do.

In Boston there was always more work to do. Sometimes growing up in Dublin seemed like a dream of an imaginary, playful childhood, and Katie had to pinch herself to remember her chores at home and the work looking after neighbor children and the late nights Mama sat up sewing by dim candlelight to bring in extra pennies. Where was the new life Mama had promised they would find? Maybe people in the New World treated them better, but their lives here still held hard work, only different tasks.

After they finished with the rugs and put them back on the wooden floors, Mama dragged the fine, polished furniture, the like of which Katie had never seen before, into place in the parlor. As a final touch, Mama threw out the old flowers, carefully wiped the delicate china bowl, and filled it with the fresh flowers that Mistress had brought in earlier. Then she cooked supper and served it to the Bentons. Katie was almost too tired to eat her own meal in the kitchen.

That night, Master Benton read the newspaper aloud, instead of reading prayers as he usually did. Katie rocked Sarah so she wouldn't cry, and the baby smiled sleepily up at her. Mistress Benton sat by the fire, sewing a dress for Sarah, while Mama mended the family's clothes. Now that her baby was quiet and happy, Mistress was calmer. She stitched fine curtains and embroidered linens for the house and spent hours helping families in town; yet she always had a smile and a kind word for Katie and Mama. Katie thought she might enjoy working for her, if only Master weren't so fierce.

Katie was only half listening until Master Benton thrust the paper into the crackling fire, shouting, "I cannot believe the royal governor refuses to see sense! We should not have to pay unfair taxes on the tea we drink. It is his job to make King George see reason."

The baby's eyes flew open at her father's loud voice, and she let out a startled shriek. *"Hush little sister,"* Katie sang softly and Sarah relaxed once more.

Mistress Benton looked at her husband. "Have you not said that the governor is servant to the king?" she asked gently. "Perhaps if we want fair treatment here, we colonials must show the king ourselves."

He glared at her for a moment, then his eyes softened and he chuckled. "Well, you're right about the governor." Then he frowned again. "But I do not know what we can do to get the king's attention, short of calling out the militia to fight his soldiers."

Mistress Benton looked down at her neat sewing. "I pray that will not happen," she said softly, "but if it does, it seems to me that fair treatment is a cause worth standing up for."

Master Benton looked at his long rifle hanging on pegs above the fireplace. "It may come to more than standing up for fair treatment," he said thoughtfully. "If the king refuses to listen, I fear it may come to fighting for independence." When Mistress didn't answer, he knelt down and banked the fire for the night.

Katie knew that Mama dreamed of independence, but she had said nothing about fighting for it. As Katie helped Mistress Benton put Sarah into her cradle, she envied Mistress's calm at the thought of fighting for a belief. Didn't she realize that if Master Benton fought the soldiers, he risked dying? Perhaps Mistress had never lost anyone, the way Katie and Mama had lost Da, and she didn't realize the danger. Much as she feared and disliked Master, Katie didn't want Sarah to lose her father.

After Mama made the kitchen ready for an early breakfast, she and Katie went to their room. "What will happen to us if the militia is called out and Master Benton goes to fight?" Katie asked the moment Mama shut the door behind them. "What if he is killed?" she asked in a smaller voice.

"Why, Mistress Benton and baby Sarah would need us all the more, Katie girl," Mama told her. "And if the colonial militias defeat the British soldiers, then the independence I've hoped and prayed for may truly happen. 'Tis why we've come to the New World."

"But it won't make any difference to us," Katie told her. "We'll still be servants—we won't be independent."

"We won't always be indentured servants," Mama said seriously. "One day, we'll be free, too. And you'll be glad to be in a free land when the terms of our indenture are up."

Katie found that almost impossible to imagine. "Will we truly be free one day? Or is that another one of your dream songs?"

"We'll truly be free," promised Mama.

"Maybe," said Katie. She snuggled close to Mama in the bed

they shared, and Mama hugged her the way she had back in Ireland, when Katie had snuggled in between Mama and Da. Softly, so she wouldn't disturb the Bentons, Mama sang.

Hush little daughter, go to sleep,
Mama's got dreams that you're gonna keep.
A house for the Reillys one fine day,
a yard where Katie can run and play.

Katie yawned. She could almost imagine Da smiling down on them. If he were still alive, she thought he'd want to fight for independence, too, no matter how risky it was. And he wouldn't complain about the hard work, either. "If a job's worth doing, it's worth the effort to do it well," he'd always told them. Katie thought Da would like the idea of working through their indenture to earn a home of their own.

"Even if it's just a lullabye," she told Mama, "it makes a nice dream."

But the next afternoon, as Katie swept the stoop, baby Sarah cried louder than ever. It was hard to remember dreams in the midst of work. "Everyone here works so hard," she complained. "No one has time to play with the baby."

Mama said, "Go rock her, and play. It will be good for you both."

Katie smiled and pushed the broom into a corner. She ran through the front room toward the cradle.

"Watch out!" cried Master Benton. He had come in from town unexpectedly, the day's paper open in his hands as he studied the news.

Katie skidded to one side, trying not to bump Master. Beneath her, the rug slid on the smooth wooden floor, and Katie crashed into the polished table. The delicate china bowl teetered. Then it fell to the floor and smashed.

"Katie!" gasped Mama.

Katie stared at the splinters of china scattered in a puddle of wet flowers. She could never mend the bowl.

"My wife's mother gave that to us on our wedding day," said Master Benton, his voice icy. "My wife brought it all the way from England. And you have broken it."

In the background, Sarah screamed.

"I'm sorry," whispered Katie.

Master Benton refolded the newspaper. "I have put up with the noise and bother of another child in the house, but this is too much."

"Please—" Mama began. She looked frightened. Katie knew they could not hope to pay for the fancy china with the little money Mama had set aside.

Master Benton held up his hand. "I said the girl could stay on trial," he told her. "The trial is over. The girl's indenture must be sold."

Mistress Benton came in, a shopping basket of dry goods on one arm. She glanced toward the cradle, then looked at Master Benton.

"What's the matter?" she asked, her voice tight with worry.

"I'm sorry," Katie whispered to her.

"There is to be a meeting this evening to decide what to do about the tea ships in the harbor," said Master Benton. "I came back to tell you I must sup early to attend it"—his eyes wandered to his long rifle above the fireplace—"and perhaps to take action, if the news at the meeting is not good. The girl was running wild through the house and broke your china bowl. I told her she must leave."

The broken pieces of china blurred as Katie's eyes filled with tears.

Sarah wailed in her lonely cradle.

"Please, may I go to her?" Katie made herself ask.

"No," said Master Benton. "Get your things to leave."

Mistress Benton touched his arm. "Let her go to the baby," she said.

Katie slipped past the Master. She lifted Sarah out of her cradle. "Hush now," she crooned. "You have to learn to be quiet. Soon you'll be all alone here, and I'll be alone in a strange house." Her voice caught, and she had to clear her throat. "I'll miss you, Sarah," she whispered, "almost as much as Mama." The idea took her by surprise. She hadn't realized that Sarah had already made a home in her heart.

The baby cried as if she understood that her world was changing. Her wailing drowned out Mistress's low voice and Master's angry one. Katie couldn't hear Mama at all. She felt like crying with Sarah. Instead, she sang. It was almost Mama's song, but it was her song, too.

Hush little sister, don't you weep.
Katie's gonna hold you until you sleep.

Bitterly, Katie wondered what Sarah had to cry about, anyway. She was lucky. She had two parents and a safe home that no one would ever turn her out of. Katie sang on, keeping her voice low, not to draw attention to herself. She added to the verse:

My da, he died in misery.
We sailed alone across the sea.
Now little sister, smile and crow.
Your ma and your da both love you so.
All your dreams, all the things you do,
Remember Katie's song for you.

Sarah's eyes were closed now, and her breathing had steadied so that Katie could hear the faint voices in the front room. She couldn't make out their words, but she knew they were deciding her future.

"You won't remember," Katie told the sleeping baby as she laid her back into the cradle, "because you'll grow up alone. I'll be working in someone else's house." Her fingers tightened on the cradle's rim. It wasn't fair! What good did a song do if it only told you what you already knew?

Was that why Mama sang her dreams? Could putting your dreams into a song help you see what you really wanted? Could it help you make it happen?

What did she want from this strange New World? She didn't want to lose Sarah, or the Mistress, but she didn't know how to hold on to them. Slowly at first, Katie began to sing again, her voice gaining strength:

Yes, little sister, sleeping there,
Katie's got dreams that you're gonna share.
A home to build in a land that's free,
A friend named Sarah to dream with me.

A shadow fell across the cradle, and Katie looked up, startled to see Mistress Benton. She'd thought the adults were still talking in the front room. "'Tis only a song, mistress," she said quickly. "I'll get my things to go."

Mistress blinked hard, as if tears blurred her sight. She said, "Stay, child."

Master Benton looked confused. "But your china—"

Mistress shook her head. Still looking at Katie, she said, "The china bowl is the past we left behind us in England—a lovely ornament like a king's crown, but no real use here." She looked up at her husband. "Sarah is our future in this New World. Sarah loves Katie, so the girl belongs here with her. You would willingly fight the king's soldiers to see us treated fairly in this new country. Would you treat Sarah's friend as unfairly as the king would treat us?"

Master Benton looked at Katie as if he hadn't really seen her before. "No," he said thoughtfully. "I would not." Behind him, Mama sighed in relief. Master Benton went on, "Soon Sarah will be out of her cradle. With two children running about the house, perhaps I should not read while I walk."

Katie saw now that he was smiling slightly—and not just at his wife and daughter. He was smiling at her, too.

Mistress patted Katie's shoulder. "May it all happen, child, just as you have sung."

Rocking Sarah gently, Katie smiled up at Mama. That was what she had meant about the New World being full of possibilities, wasn't it? It didn't guarantee that life would be easy, but it promised you the freedom to try for your dreams.

"It will happen," Katie promised Mistress, and Mama—and herself.

Twelve

by Donna Jo Napoli

I've always known I was a girl.
It doesn't matter that they call me
   tomboy
   for climbing trees
      catching lizards
         making bows and arrows from palm fronds on empty lots.
It doesn't matter that they warn me
   only boys
   like math
   build birdhouses
   argue about the infallibility of the Pope with the grown
      men who play poker with my father.
It doesn't matter because I've always known.

But I look in the mirror now
And I see something they will recognize, sooner or later:
my outside changes.
   It's not a metamorphosis
   not like a tadpole becoming a frog
   but it's not just getting bigger, either,
   not just a teeny turtle turning into a big one.
I'm a little woman, a girl grown, or growing.

They will see. They will know. They will finally accept
I'm a girl, no matter.

As for me, I've always known.
My body may be lumpy and clumsy
but my head
oh, my head is full of grace.
It always has been.
It always will be.

Flying Free

by June Rae Wood

I saw the Sleepy Eyes Motel sign flashing VACANCY in neon, and right away my stomach twisted. This early in the afternoon, the motel parking lot was empty, but on the other side of the highway, farm trucks and big rigs had crowded in at the Esso gas station and the Knife and Fork Diner. My sweaty hair felt like wet rags on the back of my neck, and the smell of hot asphalt and diesel exhaust made me want to puke.

"I'm gonna be sick," I croaked.

Dad hit the brakes on the Studebaker and swerved off the blacktop. I hung out the door and heaved in the ditch.

"Joretta? You okay?" Dad asked.

Leaning back in the seat, I shook my head and tried one last time to change his mind. "Please, Dad, let me stay with you. Don't leave me here with Aunt Wanda."

"Joretta, don't," he said, his knuckles white on the steering wheel.

"But, Dad—"

"Don't."

I glared at him, then pulled down the visor mirror to check my face. The sandy-haired, freckled girl staring back at me had a string of slobber on her cheek. I mopped myself off with a tissue and whomped the visor back in place.

"This is just for the summer, hon," Dad said.

Just for the summer? A summer could seem endless, and I should know, seeing as how I'd gotten polio and spent all of *last* summer lying flat on my back in the hospital. I'd been fed and bathed and fussed over for so long, it was hard learning to do for myself when I went home. That was the summer of 1953, one of the hottest on record in Leeway, Missouri. Yet parents wouldn't even let their kids swim in the city pool or drink from public water fountains, for fear they'd catch polio, too.

Dad reached over and patted my hand. "Might not even be the whole summer, Jo. Might be just a few weeks." When I didn't respond, he said, "Try to see my side of it. I can't expect the boss to give me short runs forever. He did it this week as a favor, but I've got to get back on the road."

"So take me with you. I like riding in that big old truck."

"You'd be bored stiff on the long hauls. Look, hon, I can't take you with me, and I can't have you staying at home by yourself. You're only twelve years old and delicate besides."

"*Delicate* means 'nervous,' like Mama. Me, I'm just plain *crippled*."

Dad cringed, and I felt a grim satisfaction. Still, I tugged at the skirt of my blue gingham dress, pulling it down as far as I could to hide my shriveled legs. Mama had already let the hem out as far as it would go. The memory caused a stinging in my eyes and throat. Letting down the hems in my summer dresses was the last thing she'd done for me before she up and took off to who-knew-where. Probably as far as *she* could go.

I'd thought the pain of polio was bad, but it didn't hold a

candle to the pain of losing Mama. Dad wanted me to think she needed a break from the two of us and had gone off somewhere to rest, but he could never look me in the eye and say that. He hadn't called the police, either, though she'd been gone for almost a week. Since he couldn't say for sure where she was, none of it made any sense. That's why the deep-down part of me knew she'd left because she couldn't stand to look at her gimpy-legged daughter.

I stared glumly at the floorboards, at my thin legs in their braces, at my clunky black shoes. I could walk better with just my left leg in a brace, but the doctor insisted I wear the right brace, too. He said that would force me to use both legs equally and not overwork the stronger side. But how would he know? Had he ever tried walking with cages on his legs?

I swallowed hard and wished fervently that I were back home, sitting on our porch swing. Already I missed hearing the creak of the chains, breathing the scent of our neighbor's roses, and tasting the icy sweetness of a cherry Popsicle on my tongue. Little things, yes, but comforting to me, especially now that this big thing with Mama was eating me alive.

I'd noticed a change in her lately. Had caught her several times just staring off into space. Then, on my last day of school, I'd come home to find Dad waiting instead of Mama. She was gone. No note, no explanation, no good-bye.

The Studebaker was moving again, bumping along on the shoulder. "I'll come and visit you when I can," Dad said as he turned into the driveway by the VACANCY sign.

"No, you won't. You'll be out looking for Mama." I wanted him to find her, of course, but I wanted to be in on the search, not stuck here in Bullpen, Missouri. This was Mama's hometown, but her parents had died before I was born, and it made her sad to come here. For sure, there wasn't much to see—just this main drag and a few back streets. Throw in her bossy sister Wanda, proud owner of the Sleepy Eye Motel, and Mama had plenty of reasons for staying away.

My gaze swept the motel—nine stone cabins with the one in the center marked OFFICE. The door of cabin number six was propped open with a maid's cleaning cart, and the TV was blaring a toothpaste jingle: "You'll wonder where the yellow went when you brush your teeth with Pepsodent!"

I sat tight, waiting for Dad to come around and help me out of the car. If he was going to dump me off, I was going to make him work at it.

In the air-conditioned office, we found Aunt Wanda doing paperwork behind the counter. It pained me to see her because she so closely resembled Mama. Same dark brown hair. Same arched eyebrows. Same dimpled chin. But the similarities ended there. Mama was a meadowlark; Aunt Wanda was a hoot owl.

She peered at us through her cat-eye glasses, then yanked them off and stood up fast when she recognized Dad and me. She seemed as stiff and unbending as her lacquered hairdo, and her gardenia scent was much too strong. "Joretta," she said, "that dress is too long, and you're skinny as a rail."

"Hello to you, too," grunted Dad.

She gave him the look that said truck drivers were common folk unless they were paying customers at the Sleepy Eye. "Joseph Barnett, why'd you wait so long to call and tell me Emma Fay was gone? My own sister!"

He shrugged. "Didn't know what to say."

"You might have asked if I'd seen her. You haven't even filed a Missing Persons Report. Tell me why I shouldn't call the police myself."

Dad scratched his ear. "Because Emma Fay's my wife, and I know her better than anybody else. I'll handle this my own way. I need time, is all."

"I can't believe she did this," huffed Aunt Wanda. "It's not just a little case of nerves this time. I think she's lost her mind."

What a horrible thing to say! I wanted to slap her, and I could see Dad felt the same way. Maybe now he wouldn't leave me here.

"Wanda," he said in a strained voice, "this is hard enough for Joretta. Please don't make it worse."

"Well, *I* didn't create the problem, but—oh, let's not get into that." Aunt Wanda glanced at her watch. "I'm on duty here for another couple of hours. Why don't you take Joretta's belongings on over to the house? I set up a bed for her in the den."

"In the *den?*" I squeaked, picturing the room with its wide archway instead of a door.

"Yes, the den. You know all my bedrooms are upstairs. With those leg braces, you're apt to tumble down the staircase, head over heels, and I'm not willing to take the risk."

Neither was I. Stairways were like mountains to me, but I had another room in mind. "Couldn't I bunk in your sewing room?"

"No, you could not. It's got all those windows, and I need the light. I'm hand-beading the bridal gown for a wedding next month."

"But I—"

"Enough," said Aunt Wanda, cutting me off. "Joretta, I don't believe children should argue with their elders. I'm sorry for your condition, but don't expect me to coddle you. Your mother's already done too much of that."

I bit my lip to keep from spouting off. What could Aunt Wanda, who'd never gotten married, possibly know about coddling a child? I glanced at Dad, hoping he'd jump to my defense, but he said nothing. From the look on his face, I had a sneaking suspicion that he agreed with Aunt Wanda. For the first time, I felt a twinge of guilt. Mama *had* coddled me to the point of exhausting herself.

Ten minutes later, my suitcases unloaded, Dad hugged me hard at Aunt Wanda's front door. "Wish it didn't have to be like this, hon. I'll call once a week and stop in when I can."

After he was gone, I returned to the den. Dens are supposed to be cozy, but this one was cramped with extra furniture—a bed in front of the fireplace, a dresser in front of the bookshelves. I hated it. The one thing it didn't have was a door.

With a sigh, I wandered outside and sat on the porch, my legs dangling over the edge, my braces thunking against the concrete. When Mama was a little girl, there'd been a big front yard with a clear view to the highway, but that was before the Sleepy Eye. I stared across the alley at the rear of the motel, at the nine cabins hulking like big blocks of stone.

As my gaze settled on the smoldering burn barrel, the summer stretched before me, as vague and shadowy as the smoke. I had nothing to do and nobody to do it with. Not much different from home, I mused, remembering how the kids at school had seemed so distant when I'd returned to class in January. Even my old friends weren't all that friendly anymore.

Not that I cared. Why should I listen to chitchat about boys and skating parties? No boy would look twice at a girl wearing braces. And forget the skates. I could fall down walking.

"Just call me Grace," I muttered, swatting at an irritating fly.

The cleaning lady came out the back door of a cabin, waved at me, and dumped some trash into the barrel. The flames leaped up, and in that instant, an idea leaped into my brain. What if Mama was hiding in Aunt Wanda's upstairs?

How silly. Mama wouldn't come here.

Would she?

She might, if she had no place else to go.

But what about Aunt Wanda? She'd the same as called Mama crazy.

Maybe that was just an act. They were sisters, after all. If she believed Mama needed a rest from *coddling* me, wouldn't she let her have a room upstairs?

Suddenly, I knew I'd have to climb those stairs somehow. With fumbling fingers, I unstrapped the brace from my right leg, put my shoe back on, and pushed myself to my feet. Soon I was in the house, gripping the banister and setting first my right foot and then the other on the bottom step. Awkward, but determined, I kept going—stronger leg, weaker leg—until I'd hauled myself to the top of the staircase.

Eyeing the empty hallway, I stood still, panting and mopping sweat from my face with the hem of my skirt. As my breathing slowed, I mentally mapped out my strategy. I intended to peek under every bed and poke my head in every closet.

However, it didn't take long for me to see I'd made that climb for nothing. Just by standing in the doorways, I could tell no one had been in the extra bedrooms lately. The frilly bedspreads were smooth; and every pillow, doll, lamp, and figurine seemed perfectly in place. Except for Aunt Wanda's room, which smelled of gardenias, all the rooms had an unused, musty odor. There wasn't a trace of Mama's lilac scent.

Feeling foolish and defeated, I leaned against the wall in the hallway, dreading the long trip down. Maybe I could scoot on my rump. Or maybe not. All those bumpety-bumps . . .

"Joretta, are you all right?"

The unfamiliar voice from below startled me, and I jerked away from the wall.

"Joretta? If you don't answer me, I'm coming in."

I inched forward to peer down the staircase. A tall, frizzy-haired girl in a pink shirt and shorts was standing at the front door, her nose mashed against the screen. Aunt Wanda must have sent her to check up on me. How else would she know my name? "I'm okay," I called, though that was a lie.

"Are you sure? You sound sort of quivery and far away. You didn't fall or anything?"

Not yet, I thought, but I resented this girl for asking. "What business is it of yours? Who are you, anyway?"

"I'm Trixie Cole, and I live down the street. I'm thirteen and nosy, so I hear things. That's how I know about the polio."

"Did Aunt Wanda send you?"

"No, and she'd have a conniption fit if she caught me peeking in this door. So I'm coming in, okay?" Without waiting for an answer, Trixie darted inside, blinking at the change from sunlight. "Whoa. How'd you get up there? No, that's a stupid question. *Why'd* you go up there?"

"I was looking for something."

"Your mother, I'll bet."

I gaped at her.

"I put two and two together," said Trixie, ascending the stairs. "Soon as I heard your mom disappeared, I started thinking how easy it would be to hide her in this house. Didn't you ever read *Jane Eyre*?"

"No."

Trixie grinned. "There's this lunatic wife locked in the attic. It'll give you the creeps." She looked me over, then looked at the stairs. "Going down's gonna be trickier than going up. Can you do it?"

"I'm not helpless."

"Didn't say you were, but it's a long ways to fall."

"Oh, really?" I said with a heavy dose of sarcasm.

"Hey, don't get your back up. I'm here to help."

"So you *do* think I'm helpless. Go away, Trixie. I'll figure it out."

"Well, aren't you Miss Suzy Sunshine?" Trixie gave a little snort and started back the way she'd come.

Looking down, I felt a surge of panic. "Trixie, wait!"

She stopped and turned to eyeball me. "You rang?"

"I—uh—would you come back up? Let me lean on you?"

"I could do that, but I've got a better idea. Why not slide down the banister?"

"You're not serious," I said, shocked.

"Oh, yes, I am. It's the quickest way down."

"But that's dangerous."

"Hey, don't be a scaredy-cat. With me engineering, you'll be all right."

I was tempted. Most people pitied me. I could see it in their eyes. But here was Trixie, practically daring me to give her idea a try.

"Here's how we'll do it," she said. "I'll boost you up, you hang on till I get to the bottom, and I'll catch you. Nothing to it."

That brought a smile to my face. "You won't think 'nothing to it' if you have to tell Aunt Wanda I've slid to my death."

Trixie smiled back. "Sounds to me like you're ready to launch."

Both of us giggling the whole time, I slid down the banister—whee! Trixie caught me and settled me on my feet.

"Thanks," I said. "I've always wanted to do that."

We burst out laughing and headed outside to the porch, where we plunked ourselves down in lawn chairs.

Trixie stooped over to pick up my leg brace and handed it to me. She watched as I put it back on. "When I first saw that thing, empty, it kinda spooked me. It was like you'd been zapped up into a flying saucer. You know, like on TV."

"We don't have a TV."

"Neither do we, but I watch at my neighbor's house. And my mom's the maid at the Sleepy Eye, so I watch in the cabins when she's cleaning up."

"Aunt Wanda doesn't care?"

"Why should she care? I don't just sit around while my shows are on. I have to change sheets and dust furniture, and that saves your aunt money. With two of us working, Mom gets done quicker."

"Do you come every day?"

"Does the sun rise every morning?"

I smiled to myself. Already I didn't feel quite so lonely.

"Wish I could help you find your mom," Trixie said.

"Me, too. It's like a bad dream."

She nodded. "I'll bet. If Sergeant Friday was here, he'd solve the case. I'm talking about that *Dragnet* show."

"We get that on the radio."

"'Just the facts, ma'am,'" Trixie growled, mimicking the sergeant's no-nonsense voice.

Just the facts. I shifted uneasily in my chair. Should I tell Trixie the facts about Mama? It didn't seem right to discuss family matters with a stranger. But I'd been aching to talk to somebody, and my need for that won out. I drew a deep breath and said, "Trixie, the police wouldn't be interested in Mama's case. She made up her own mind to leave. I know it. Dad knows it. Even Aunt Wanda knows it. Otherwise, she'd have called the police whether Dad wanted her to or not."

Trixie popped her knuckles, giving that some thought. "Do your mom and dad fight a lot? Could she be teaching him a lesson?"

"No, Mama's not a fighter. Just the opposite, really. She's as gentle as can be. You should see her with wounded birds."

"But she left you in the lurch?" asked Trixie, incredulous.

I flinched.

"Sorry. I shouldn't have put it like that. Go on. I'll try to keep my mouth shut."

"Mama's real good at rescuing birds. Like the duck at the park whose beak was almost cut in half by a tangled fishing line, and like the robin with the broken wing. She patches them up and cares for them, and eventually they fly free."

A baffled Trixie squinted at me. "So? What's that got to do with her running off?"

"Since I came home from the hospital, she's been waiting on me, hand and foot. Bringing me Popsicles while I did my homework. Massaging my leg muscles at night. Even singing me to sleep. But look at me. I'm still crippled. I think she gave up when she couldn't fix me."

"That's nuts, Joretta. You don't stop loving somebody because they got sick. Sounds like the feel-sorries are warping your brain. What you need is a big bowl of ice cream. Let's walk over to the Knife and Fork."

I spooned in my last bite of ice cream and glanced around the diner. The place had been hopping when we wandered in, but now the rush was over. I could barely hear Kitty Wells singing on the jukebox, what with the waitress clattering dishes off the counter. "Looks like a cyclone hit," I said, eyeing the dirty plates and cups and wadded-up napkins cluttering every table.

"Yep," said Trixie. "Gertrude can't find enough help for the day shift. Here she comes now, and she looks plumb worn out."

A chubby woman had emerged from the swinging doors of the kitchen. Wearing a flowered dress, a grease-spattered apron, and a hairnet, she plodded past our booth with a tired, "Howdy, Trixie. You, too, hon." Soon she came plodding back, sipping at a glass of iced tea, and she stopped and peered down at me. "You're Emma Fay's girl."

"Yes, but how—"

"Wanda comes over for coffee at five-thirty every morning. We discuss the world's problems before I unlock the doors at six."

I smiled at the image that called up: Aunt Wanda in a bathrobe, rollers in her hair, huddling over coffee on a barstool.

Gertrude wiped moisture off her glass with her apron. "Don't reckon you girls want a job?"

"Washing dishes?" asked Trixie.

"And cleaning off tables. Wouldn't need you but just a while in the afternoons. You'd both get fifty cents an hour and all you can eat. Think it over. Talk to your folks." Sipping at her tea, Gertrude headed back to the kitchen.

"What do you say?" asked Trixie, grinning at me.

"I say I can't do it."

"Why not? You wash dishes with your hands, not your legs."

"Very funny, but you're not the one wearing braces."

"Didn't stop you from climbing those stairs."

"Not the smartest thing I've ever done."

"But you tried it. That's the important thing." With that, Trixie slid out of the booth, fetched a tray from the counter, and plopped it down in front of me. "You get the tables. I'll get the booths."

Within fifteen minutes, I loved the job. Not the steaming, soapy dishwater and the stinky bleach-water rinse. Not the mountainous jumble of greasy dishes. Not the bucket of grimy forks that had to soak before being scrubbed with a wire brush.

But I loved everything else about that job. The teamwork. Trixie's silly jokes about dishpan hands to our elbows and about sweating ourselves down to nubs. The burping and giggling as we guzzled free Cokes. The sense of victory at seeing gleaming silverware and towering stacks of spotless stoneware plates.

Eventually, Trixie and I left the diner, our bellies stuffed with french fries, our pockets jingling with three quarters each. "Wish me luck with Aunt Wanda," I said as we waited at the roadside for traffic to clear.

"She'll say yes. Gertrude needs the help, and you need something to do. Get ready. We'll go after this pickup." The truck whizzed past, and Trixie caught my hand and towed me across the blacktop.

I gazed up at the motel's VACANCY sign. So much had happened since I'd thrown up at the sight of it earlier that afternoon. "You want to know something weird?" I said. "All week long, I've thought of nothing but Mama. But I didn't think about her one time while we were slaving away on those dishes."

"My mom says there's nothing like hard work to take your mind off your troubles. Yeah, it's rough that your mother's gone and you've got leg braces, but the way I see it, you're lucky to be alive. Two years ago, my dad got polio and died."

A little "oh" whooshed out of me.

"That's why your aunt hired my—whoa!" Trixie's blue eyes widened. "I just thought of something!"

"What?"

"Maybe there's a good reason Miss Morris didn't call the police. Maybe it's right in front of us, and we're just too dumb to see it."

I blinked at her, not comprehending.

"The Sleepy Eye. Mom and I clean the cabins that got rented out overnight. We just check the register so we know which rooms need work. Somebody could be in one of the 'empty' cabins and not be in the book."

My heart flip-flopped in my chest. "Mama," I breathed, scanning the cabins.

"Don't gawk. Miss Morris might be watching from the office. Let's go back to her porch and talk."

Two minutes later, sitting on the porch, I stared at the cabins as if I could see through walls. If Mama were this close, how long would I have to pretend she wasn't? How long would she and Aunt Wanda keep the secret?

Trixie hitched her chair closer to mine. "If your mother's in there, we can find out tonight. Are you game for some detective work?"

"Like what? Peeking in windows?"

"Hey, I'm not *that* dumb. All we have to do is slip outside after dark and take a look out front. See how many cabins have lights. See how many cars are parked."

"That might not tell us anything," I said doubtfully. "What if people came in one car but rented separate cabins? The numbers wouldn't match."

"Right," agreed Trixie, "but I know the night clerk, and I'd figure out some way to peek at the reg—"

We both gave a guilty start as the screen door popped open and Aunt Wanda barreled onto the porch. "You girls have cooked up quite a scheme," she said.

The french fries I'd eaten became a big, greasy knot, weighting me to my chair. But Trixie jumped to her feet and stammered, "We—uh—were just talking—"

"I know. I heard every word. This is real life, not some TV show that always has a happy ending. We're on the highway with strangers coming and going at all hours of the night. What if somebody forced you into a car and left, and hours passed before you were even missed?"

I gulped.

Aunt Wanda drew a deep breath and cast her eyes heavenward, like maybe she was praying. "Girls, I could tell you a hundred times that Emma Fay is not at the Sleepy Eye, but who's to say you'd believe me? I'll not have you sneaking around in the dark, so let's march over there right now. You can inspect the premises in broad daylight."

"Uh, Miss Morris," said Trixie in a quaky voice, "there's no call for that. I believe you."

"How about you, Joretta?" demanded Aunt Wanda.

I managed to peep, "Me, too," though my eyes burned and a lump clogged my throat. For a little while, I'd had my hopes up again about finding Mama.

Aunt Wanda sighed. "All right, girls. There's no sense in beating this to death. It's been a long day, and it's not over yet. So Trixie, it's time for you to take that wild imagination of yours and run along home."

"Yes, ma'am." Trixie flashed me a woeful look and scurried off the porch.

"It's out of the question, Joretta," said Aunt Wanda as she dropped a pork chop into the skillet. "I'll talk to Gertrude in the morning. You can't do that job."

"I can. I *did*."

"You wouldn't last a week, once the newness wears off."

"You don't know that."

"I'd say it's a pretty good guess. You can hardly do anything for yourself, much less help anybody else."

"That's not so."

"It *is* so. You haven't unpacked your suitcases. You haven't even made your own bed."

"I'll do it now."

"You certainly will. This is not the motel, and there's no maid service here. When you finish, please come back and set the table."

I stalked away from her, only to stalk back a few minutes later, hauling my empty suitcases. "Where do these go?"

"Just set them in my sewing room. I'll have to make room in the closet."

In the sewing room, I grudgingly admired the bridal gown fanned out on the table—yards and yards of white satin, with hundreds of beads stitched to the bodice.

"Don't touch," said Aunt Wanda from the doorway.

I jerked my hand back.

"Body oils," she said.

Body oils? Only a hoot owl would worry about something like that.

"They stain the fabric, over time," she said. "It's important to wash your hands first."

"Oh." I ducked my head and brushed past her to set the table.

"Joretta? Wait."

I waited, not knowing what to expect.

"If I let you accept the job with Gertrude, you'd be committed. I wouldn't let you quit."

I stared at her. "Are you saying you changed your mind?"

"Yes."

"I'll work hard, Aunt Wanda. Honest."

In reply, she walked to the stove and checked the pork chops.

As I reached into the cabinet for dishes, she said, "There's plenty of time for that. Pull out a chair, and let's talk."

Mystified, I sat and watched her pour coffee into a dainty china cup with roses around the rim.

"I don't know how to say this," she began, sitting down, "except to just come out with it. After your father dropped you off here, he slipped back to the office and told me where your mother is."

"He *knows?*" I gasped. Never in my life had I felt so betrayed.

"He's known all along. Just didn't know what to tell you. The way it happened—the circumstances—well, he was afraid you'd think it was your fault."

"What circumstances?" I choked out.

"Your last day of school. Emma Fay at the window, watching you go. Kids everywhere, but you all alone, limping off down the sidewalk. She started crying and couldn't stop."

"Why? Because I'm crippled?"

"Because summer's a time for roller skating and riding bikes— but not for you. It broke her heart."

"She had a funny way of showing it. Running off."

"Joretta, she had a nervous breakdown. Your father took her to Reed Center."

"*The mental hospital?*" I felt all the color drain from my face.

Aunt Wanda nodded. "That's why he didn't tell a soul."

"Not even me," I muttered.

"He still doesn't think you should know. But he left you in my charge, and I can't go along with misleading you."

"Has he seen Mama?"

"She can't have visitors yet or even phone calls. That man's so beside himself, he wasn't making sense. At least, that's what I thought when he started talking about eagles. How they build their nests on a rocky ledge. How nature tells them it's do or die."

"That's something Mama read in a bird magazine," I said, impatient and angry. "What's that got to do with her breakdown?"

"I'm getting there, Joretta." Aunt Wanda took a sip of steaming coffee. "Eagles poke holes in the nest and stir things up to make it lumpy and uncomfortable when their babies are fully grown. The mother flies away with a young eagle on her back, then darts out from under him. If he falters, she swoops down and catches him. She'll do that maybe thirty or forty times, until instinct tells her to stop. She knows if he can't fly, he's not strong enough to survive."

I was beginning to get the picture, and I didn't like it. "I'm not an eagle, and Mama doesn't carry me," I said coldly.

"Of course not. She hasn't even stirred up the nest. She thinks you're not strong enough to survive."

"I survived polio."

"That's not the point. You used to be a happy little girl with lots of friends. Now you're a loner. Why is that? Could it be that your 'poor me' attitude—not the braces on your legs—is what drove your friends away?"

That's not what I wanted to hear, but I had to admit she was right. I'd had the feel-sorries for so long, I didn't even like myself much.

"Fair warning," said Aunt Wanda, tapping her nails on the table. "Your father is counting on me to stir up the nest."

She'd already started on that. Insisting I sleep in the den. Bossing me around. Complaining about body oils, for heaven's sake. But I could deal with it. I had Trixie, I had a job, and I wanted Mama back. I traced my finger along a stripe in the tablecloth. "Aunt Wanda?"

"What?"

"Do you think Mama's gonna be okay?"

Aunt Wanda stirred her coffee and looked down at the table-cloth. When she looked up, she was almost smiling.

"I think you're *both* going to be okay. Something tells me you'll be flying on your own very soon."

I blinked in surprise at her sudden kindness. Then, just to stir her up, I said, "It sure felt like I was flying when I slid down your banister today."

Her cup clattered against the saucer. "You did *what?*"

"I slid down the banister. Trixie helped me."

Aunt Wanda sagged in her chair. "I can see it now. You girls are going to be the death of me."

I couldn't help smiling as the deep-down part of me disagreed. My aunt would survive, and so would I. No, not just survive. When Mama came home, I'd be flying free.

The Apple

by Linda Sue Park

Mrs. Carter stood at the front of the room with a big basket on the table next to her. "Last project of the year," she said. "Title: 'The Apple.'"

She took an apple from the basket and held it up. "Now that may sound simple, but I want you to keep in mind some of the styles we've looked at this year. Realism, Impressionism, pointillism—let's see some creativity, people!"

I loved art class, partly because it was the only class I had with my best friend, Sarah. For a whole bunch of other reasons, too: no homework, no tests, no grades—and glitter.

In the pocket of her smock, Mrs. Carter kept a little jar of multicolored glitter with a shaker top. Every once in a while— not very often, a couple times a month at most—she'd take it out and throw a tiny bit on someone, for doing an extra-good project, or for having a really great idea even if it didn't work out in the end, or for trying hard. "You're a Glitter Guy!" she'd say, or "Glitter Girl!" It was kind of corny, and lots of kids, especially the boys, said they hated it—the glitter got stuck in your clothes and your hair and sometimes even your eyebrows, but secretly I thought no one really minded because when you saw someone glittering in the halls or the lunchroom or the library, you knew it was because they'd done something good in Mrs. Carter's class.

I'd been a Glitter Girl just once so far. For the first project of the year, my autobiographical collage made of photos cut from magazines. Mrs. Carter said it showed "an excellent sense of the value of white space." I wasn't quite sure what she meant by that—I'd left space between some of the photos because I couldn't find very many I liked—but then she glittered me and helped me put my collage on the wall.

I didn't want to be a suck-up or anything like that, but all year I'd been trying to get glittered again. This project would be my last chance. Mrs. Reese, the seventh-grade art teacher, didn't do the glitter thing.

Mrs. Carter passed out the apples. They were different colors, red, green, yellow—I ended up with a red one.

Some kids got to work right away but not me; I wanted to think a little first. So I watched the others for a while.

Ruben took a bite of his apple and then put it down and started drawing. Sarah asked Mrs. Carter for a knife and cut hers in half and put the two halves at sort of an angle to each other and started drawing. That gave Megan an idea; she cut her apple up into a whole lot of slices. Chris must have liked Ruben's idea because he took a bite of his apple, too, a big one, but he didn't chew or swallow; instead he took the bitten-off piece out of his mouth and held it up, and we all said "EWWWW," and he laughed and put that piece next to his apple, facing where it came from, and he started to draw.

James looked over from the next table and saw what Chris was doing and said, "Cool! Mrs. Carter! Can I eat my apple but not swallow and spit out all the chewed-up bits and draw those?"

Everyone laughed and said things like *disgusting* and *gross,* and Mrs. Carter said, "Very creative, James—and we don't even get to Postmodernism until seventh grade! But I'm afraid it's not terribly sanitary, so no chewing up and spitting out, please."

James shook his head and said, "Awwww—" and Mrs. Carter sort of swooped down on him and said, "Glitter guy!" and he put his hands up over his head to shield himself but it was too late; there he was all sparkly, and everybody cheered.

I looked at James's table. James had decided to eat his apple anyway, but chew and swallow, not spit it out, and he said—as he sat there glittering—that he was going to draw just the core. And Jaya had cut hers up in slices like Megan's, but she'd arranged all the slices into a big letter *A.* She saw me looking and said, "You know those alphabet books for little kids, *A* is always for apple, right?" Wow, I really loved that. I wished I'd thought of it.

I was practically the only one not drawing. I kept trying to think of something really cool to do with my apple, something Mrs. Carter would really like. I thought about our last lesson, on perspective. We had to draw a chair from different angles, from the side and from the top and from behind. Mrs. Carter had used this deep, slow voice and boomed out, *"You—are—the— chair. BE the chair,"* and everyone had laughed. I turned my apple on its side and then upside down, but that didn't give me any good ideas either, not at first. I looked at my apple from the top again and I could see where the stem would have been if my apple had had a stem but it didn't, just a hole, and that made me wonder what it would look like if I could put my eye up to the hole and somehow see *into* the apple and that gave me another idea—

"*What* are you doing?" Sarah asked. I guess it must have looked funny, me holding the apple up to my eye like it was a telescope or something.

"I was just thinking," I said. "What if you were small enough to be inside the apple, what would it look like then?"

"I don't get it," Sarah said. "How would that work?"

"Just say you could climb down into the apple and stand in the middle, you know, in the core, facing out—what would you see?"

"Um, you'd see white, wouldn't you?" Sarah said. "All the white stuff."

Ruben snorted. "All white, that'd be a great picture," he said.

I laughed but inside I felt a little annoyed; I don't know if I was annoyed at him or annoyed that my idea wasn't working out like I'd hoped.

Sarah started laughing—she had this really great laugh, like a hyena; she was famous for it. "Lauren's going to do an all-white picture," she said, then pointed to the blank piece of paper in front of me. "Look, she's already finished," and she howled laughing.

I crossed my eyes at her. "Dork," I said, and now we were both laughing. That's the thing about being really good friends; you can tease each other and not end up mad.

We calmed down and Sarah and Ruben went back to work and I sat there *still* thinking. What they'd said about an all-white picture had given me an idea. I didn't know if it was a good idea or not, but at least it was something I could try.

My apple had a bruise on one side. I got the knife and cut the apple in half, making sure to cut right through the bruise.

Sarah looked at my apple and then at me. "You're not copying me, are you?"

"Of course not," I said, "I want mine to be *good.*"

She gave me a pretend slap. "Dweeb," she said and did the hyena thing again.

I looked at my apple—I mean, *really* looked at it. Maybe I could make this idea work. I went to the supply cupboard to get what I needed, pastel chalks and oil pastels. I took beige and brown and light green and went back again for yellow.

My picture took three classes to finish. I drew with a pencil first, over and over. I erased so much that sometimes I erased a hole in the paper. When I finally got the drawing part right, I had to fill in the colors, and it took me ages to get *those* right. I copied the drawing again and again, and I wore out two beige pastels and one brown one.

It was strange how much I got into it. All I was thinking about was how to make this idea come out right, how to draw it as best I could. Sometimes the whole room almost seemed to disappear—the buzz of the other kids and Mrs. Carter flitting around and even Sarah's laugh. It was just me and the apple and the picture, and the time flew by without it ever feeling like *work.*

I rubbed the paper with my fingertip to blur the pastel. Gently—just a little more—not too much.

OK. That was it. Finished.

I let out this big sigh; it was like I'd been holding my breath for ages. The picture on the page *finally* looked almost like the one in my head. I sat there a minute longer. Then I went to the supply cupboard for some of that tacky blue stuff.

Mrs. Carter let us decide whether to display our work. If you didn't want to, you didn't have to. She'd look at it in your folder and check off in her book that you'd done it and talk to you about it. I always waited until she talked to me, and if she didn't have hardly any suggestions for improving my project, I'd put it on the wall.

But this time was different. I wasn't sure exactly why, but I didn't want to show her first. I felt a little jittery as I rolled the tacky stuff into little balls.

Sarah watched me stick down the last corner of my picture.

"*That's* an apple?" she said.

My stomach did a flop-over thing. I took a deep breath. "It's a close-up," I said, hoping my voice didn't sound shaky. Couldn't she see what I'd tried to do?

She sort of scrunched up her face. "Well, without the caption you'd never guess it was an apple," she said. Mrs. Carter had asked us all to write "The Apple" at the bottom of our pictures. "I think it's very—um, original."

I guess I was glad she was being honest, but mostly I felt this giant wave of disappointment in my stomach. "Thanks," I forced myself to say. Then I took a few steps away from the wall and looked at my picture again.

I tried to concentrate on the shapes and colors instead of on the panicky feeling in my stomach. Should I take it down and change something? No, I'd tried a *gazillion* things—I knew it was the just the way I wanted it.

But maybe Sarah was right about one thing. . . . I thought about it a moment longer, then took a pencil and added a couple words to the caption.

Jaya came up just then and stood next to me and read what

I'd written: "'The Apple: *interior, close-up.*'" She stared at my picture for a little while. I pretended to be looking at the other projects but really I was waiting to hear if she said anything else.

Some of the pictures were great. Sarah's was sort of comic-book style, heavy black lines and bright colors. James had used pen and ink to draw his core with millions of tiny dots; it was amazing. Jaya's hadn't turned out like I'd imagined it, those slices in the shape of a letter *A*—maybe it would have been better as a photograph.

I turned toward her. "I loved your idea," I said.

She bobbed her head at me. "I'm still checking yours out. *'Interior, close-up,'*" she mumbled and frowned a little. "The pointy thing, that's part of a seed, the tip of it. And this huge blur—" she pointed to the top left corner—"a bruise, maybe? Really *really* close-up. Weird," she said and nodded.

My stomach again—only this time, a huge wave of relief. "Thanks," I said.

I was surprised to realize that it didn't matter to me if she *liked* it; I mean, maybe she hadn't meant *weird* to be a compliment. But she'd understood what those strange brown and beige shapes were! From the apple to my brain to the paper to Jaya's brain—it was like this magical invisible string you could follow.

I almost wanted to shout out loud, *"She got it, she got it!"* I had to press my lips together to keep from smiling too much. And I realized something else, too: Seventh-grade art was going to be a blast.

Even without the glitter.

Annie's Opinion

by Sheila Solomon Klass

"Rice pudding with lots of raisins," I said.

"Fresh bread with butter and blackberry jam," my little brother, John, answered quickly, licking his lips.

The two of us were home alone as usual that morning, sitting together by the cold hearth, with me, the big sister, in charge. Our four older sisters had hired out to do chores for neighbors during the day while Ma was off working as district nurse. We were a poor Quaker farm family living on the Ohio prairie, struggling because our pa had frozen to death in a winter blizzard.

This day John and I were so hungry we couldn't think of anything but food, so we were playing our favorite game.

My turn. "Roast chicken with cornbread stuffing."

"Sugared doughnuts. Apple fritters and syrup and . . ."

I stopped him. "Too many sweets, John," I said, echoing Ma. "Besides, after your doughnuts, it's my turn. Let me see . . . rabbit stew." Just then I looked through the window, and as if my words had summoned him, a big jackrabbit came bounding into our garden. Hopping all over like he'd planted it and it was his very own garden. He nibbled boldly away at our baby cabbages. It was too much for me. My eyes lighted on Pa's old rifle up on the wall. I moved a chair under it and began to climb up.

"What're you doing, Annie?" John asked nervously. "Ma said never to touch—"

I was mindful of what she'd said, and I was terrified. The only thing sharper than my fear was the two years of hunger since Pa had died. It just seemed to me that rabbit had been sent there for me. "I'm going to get us a rabbit for dinner."

"Oh, no, Annie!"

"Hold my feet steady," I ordered, and he obediently wrapped his arms tight around my legs.

Carefully, I did what was forbidden. I took the heavy gun down, barely able to manage its weight. Dumbstruck, John watched as I first rubbed and polished the rifle, then greased it. I remembered what Pa always said about respecting your gun, and I worked hard at doing that.

I'd listened to him and watched him load so many times, I just did as he said. "First you measure the powder carefully and pour it in and tamp it down. Then add the shot." All the while my head was singing its own little song:

Rabbit stew, rabbit stew.

Plenty for you and you and you.

I could already smell the gravy. I could taste the sweet carrots and see the tender white chunks of meat.

Pointing the barrel upward the way Pa used to, with John helping to support the weighty stock, together we lugged that big gun outside. "Take cover far from me," I ordered, and he scampered away, leaving me crouching there quietly. *Oh, let me get it exactly right.* I stayed put a long time till that rabbit headed for the cucumbers—his next course. Then I pulled the trigger, and I got him on the first shot, which was just as well because I'd put too much powder in the gun. It practically jumped out of my hands and knocked me down.

"Annie!" Johnny began to wail. "Ma said never to touch the gun. Oh, Annie, I'm only six. What'll I do if you're dead? You were such a good sister."

I lay there breathing hard and trying not to giggle as I let him go on about how wonderful I was. Then I raised up from the ground on my elbows and spooked him. "Yaah!" I shouted, making him jump.

I was very proud of shooting that rabbit, and Johnny was even prouder as soon as he realized that I was all right.

But Ma was furious and scolded me roundly as soon as she got home. You wouldn't think a Quaker could get so riled up. Quakers are supposed to be peaceful, quiet people.

"You could have killed yourself—or John," she pointed out sternly. "Or done some terrible injury. And—you disobeyed me." She paused a while to let that sink in. "You know very well that girls don't shoot."

"But they do, Ma. I did. I shot that rabbit clean through the head."

"She did, Ma. I seen her." John backed me up.

"Saw, John. Not seen." Ma paused, tightlipped. "I know she did. It's very hard to believe Annie's that skilled. She's got a most peculiar talent. A boy's talent." Ma shook her head as if to clear it.

Till that moment nobody had ever said I had any talent at all. When I sewed, my running stitches couldn't even walk in a straight line, and when I helped with the baking, the biscuits always burned. As for singing, well, I liked to sing but Ma hushed me whenever the family all sang together. She said that the others, Lydia, Mary Jane, Elizabeth, and Sarah Ellen, had sweet voices, but I threw everybody off.

"Off where?" I asked, looking around. We lived in the village of North Star, a very flat place, and besides, during singing I never did anything. I sang loud, but I stood still.

Ma was like that. "You always throw everybody off," was all she'd say. Pa used to explain things clear so I understood, but when I had only Ma to look to, she never explained. She was a doer, she said, and not a talker or dreamer. She left things to be figured out.

Ma kept on her scolding, all the while staring down at the dead rabbit. "Annie, you should not have done this dangerous thing. It's strange and not seemly for a girl."

"We gonna eat that rabbit, Ma?" I asked nervously. I'd die if she was so cross with me that she'd end up throwing away the rabbit. I was so hungry. Being hungry makes you good at things. It made me good at setting little string snares in the fields for grouse and quail and small animals, which I caught occasionally, and now it had made me good at shooting, and it made me real good at eating, too. I had learned to eat just about anything.

"Yes, we'll eat the rabbit. I can't waste good food," Ma said, "but don't do it ever again. Girls don't shoot."

We had a great feast that evening: the rabbit cooked in butter and parsley with carrots and wild mushrooms, turnips, and green beans, and mashed potato mountains with little gravy streams dribbling down them and then berry pies, flaky and golden. My sisters and my brother all looked so happy and talked so much at the table, it was almost like old times when Pa was alive. Mary Jane, my favorite sister, hit her spoon up against her glass, and when everyone was quiet she said, "Three cheers for Annie!" And my sisters and brother shouted, "Hip, hip, hooray!" Not Ma, though. She was busy clearing dishes.

Once I knew how easy it was for me to shoot, it got harder and harder to sit around hungry staring at Pa's gun on the wall and knowing that there was all that food running around outdoors. All of us children worked in the garden growing vegetables; we gathered nuts, and we berried, but there was never enough to eat. Still, she was my ma and I had to heed her words. Girls didn't shoot. Shooting was unwomanly, and I would grow up to be a woman. So for a very long time I held back.

But things only got worse. I was so hungry, my stomach made growling noises all day long, and I had a hard time sleeping at night. Our clothes hung loose on us; we looked as ragged as scarecrows. We felt tired a lot of the time. So I worked out a plan. I'd teach John to shoot. Since he was a boy, it was okay for him to hunt us some food. Ma was willing to let me use my peculiar gift to teach him so long as we were very careful with the gun. Very, very careful. I guess Ma was hungry, too, though she never let on.

Well, John did his best. We went out into the fields and the woods each morning and we practiced shooting at targets and small game, but he just didn't have a good enough eye. He was so eager he ended up squeezing that trigger much too hard. After many misses, he was sometimes right on the edge of crying, though he held back. I could see we weren't getting any closer to food, and the shooting lessons were making John feel terrible, so we stopped them. "Maybe when you're older," I said, "then you'll have a better eye."

"You really think so, Annie?" He did so want to help.

I nodded to cheer him, but I knew John wasn't a shooter.

On the morning of my tenth birthday, I was desperate. I couldn't bear the idea of going hungry on my birthday. "Johnny," I whispered, "what would you say to roast turkey? Or duck? Or goose?"

His eyes brightened. "Are we playing our game?"

I shook my head. I was so terrified at what I was about to propose that my voice was practically gone. "I will shoot us some food, and we'll tell Ma you shot it. She won't know."

"That's telling a lie, Annie," he whispered back.

"Don't I know that?"

"Lying is worse than sh-shooting." He was trembling.

"Who says?" I was bolder now. Once I'd actually said the words, I'd taken a big step toward doing the deed. "You don't have to say the lie out loud. You just be quiet. I'll do the lying."

John thought about it.

"I'll get us a game bird or some rabbits. Come on, John."

He thought more about it, and though he was mighty scared, he was mighty hungry, too.

"All right," he agreed, "but I'm not lying."

I nodded.

As soon as Ma and the others left for work, I took the rifle down again and loaded it. Then I pulled a sack on over my dress to keep off the burrs and I set out.

It was a mild, gorgeous day, the sky a soft blue and the sun smiling down on me. My heart pounded with excitement and guilt. I was not a liar; I tried to tell the truth to everyone. And the one person, more than any other, to whom I owed the truth was Ma. I was aware of all that and I carried it on my conscience, but it didn't stop me.

I made my way along quietly, scouting, watching all around me.

Come out, come out, you're my birthday treat.

You've got to come out, you're our dinner meat.

The rhyme hummed round and round inside my head as I positioned myself silently. I stayed very still and kept my breathing quiet. After a while there was a small stirring in the brush. Then a wild turkey scurried out, flapping its big wings. Smoothly curving my arm up and around in a single motion the way Pa used to, I lifted the gun and focused so I saw and heard nothing but that turkey. There was only me and that bird in the whole world. Me and that big, beautiful, birthday Tom turkey.

I shot and brought it down.

It was a very large bird, too heavy to carry. I took off the sack I was wearing and put the turkey in there so I could drag it home.

Johnny was waiting on the porch.

"You shot a big turkey, John," I called to him, busting with pride.

"Oh, no, Annie!" was all he could moan.

"You sure know which birds to go after," I grinned, loving that I was teasing him.

"Oh, no!"

"Oh, yes, John."

He disappeared into the house, leaving me to wait for Ma. I just sat there. Jubilant and worried. Smiling and scared.

After a while, Ma came driving up in the wagon.

"'lo, Ma," I called, and, leaving the turkey on the porch, I ran to help her unhitch the horse and lead him into the barn.

"Johnny's . . . Johnny's shot a wild turkey," I said, my voice scratchy.

"What?"

I stopped breathing.

Ma didn't say a word. She slowly picked her way up the front path to the porch, and then she stooped over and dumped the turkey out of the sack.

"Johnny shot this turkey?"

"Yes, Ma."

She turned and looked at me with the saddest eyes. "Annie, who shot this turkey?"

"J-Johnny."

"I will only ask you once more, child. Your pa and I taught you to speak the truth. Who shot this turkey?"

I fell apart before her accusing eyes. "Ma—Ma, it's my birthday and I was so hungry and I'm such a good shooter and it's not fair that girls can't shoot if they have a talent. I know it's a peculiar talent 'cause you said so, but—Ma—I can feed us, Ma. I can take care of us."

I was weeping now, and a few tears ran down Ma's cheeks, too. Taking a step back from me, she stood looking down.

"Hush," she said, "hush. I understand, child. I do. I hate that you have to shoot to feed us." She shut her eyes and swallowed deep. "But you're a good child, and I know that it is not your habit to lie. I know you will not lie again." Her words were kind enough, but she stood there stiff and still and her tone was unforgiving.

I longed for her to embrace me and say it was all right, but I knew Ma could never hug a girl who shot a gun.

Through my sniffling I heard the floorboards creak and I

sensed that John was right inside the doorway with his ear pressed against the crack, trying to figure out what was happening. "That's Johnny," I said. "It was my idea, Ma. He didn't want to lie. He was hungry, too."

"John," she called, "come out here."

Slowly, he tiptoed out as if he were hoping he might find us asleep. Ma reached out to him and stroked his hair. "I know Annie shot the turkey," she said. "You are both good children." He hugged her around the waist gratefully, and she drew him close to her. Ma forgave us both, but she forgave him more because he was a boy.

"It is just so strange," she said, "that Annie was blessed with the skill you should have, John. Who knows? She may have been sent to care for us." With that, Ma bent over and reached for the turkey to lug it into the house. "Well"—she sighed softly—"if Annie's peculiar talent provides food, then we must be thankful for what we receive. So be it."

Those last words set me free forever to use my skill—even if Ma thought it was a mistake. I became a market hunter, selling the game I shot to merchants. I was good. Really good. I paid off the mortgage on the family farm before I was fifteen years old, and I supported my sisters and brother, and Ma as long as she lived.

But she didn't hug me on my birthday or even stroke my hair or touch my shoulder. That was because Ma believed her whole life long in doing only what was fitting. So she couldn't rightly love a daughter who was a shooter.

Even if that daughter turned out to be the most famous sharpshooter in the world: me, Annie Oakley.

Who has never once used a gun against a human being.

Who can hold a rifle on her shoulder backward, look into a mirror, and shoot glass balls tossed up in the air behind her.

Who can shoot holes in playing cards and in nickels held up at a distance between thumb and forefinger.

Who can hit targets shooting from the back of a galloping horse.

Who can shoot the ash off the cigarette in her husband's mouth!

A woman who can do all that. Who was applauded in London by the Prince of Wales and even Queen Victoria herself.

I believe a person is blessed if she's real good at one thing. I believe that person should be allowed to use her special talent, whatever it is, and be honored for it. Yes, honored. And not just honored.

Hugged, too.

Princess Isobel and the Pea—
A Love Story in Five Chapters

by Valiska Gregory

CHAPTER ONE

When Princess Isobel arrived at the castle,
the prince warned her about the mattresses.
She even knew about the queen's test
with the pea hidden hard as an emerald underneath,
though how a dried-up pea could possibly prove
she was a real princess was anybody's guess.
Still, she took a book and read far into the night
and then she slipped into a morning dream
blue as a crocus, so that when she awoke
she was just sleepy-eyed enough to satisfy the queen.
"You're not a natural beauty," the queen said,
"but we have hair spray. We have persimmon rouge."

CHAPTER TWO

Isobel's shoes were too tight, her lipstick too red,
but the queen told her the illusion was perfect.
The courtiers admired her delicate yellow satin
and they didn't even notice when she deftly
hid a slight daffodil yawn behind her glove.
Like wallpaper flowers, they repeated her every pattern

until one day, quite deliberately, she tripped on a rug
just to see if they would follow, and of course they all did.
She expected them at any moment to *baa* like sheep.
What Isobel *didn't* know before she came to the castle
was just how those pinched royal slippers would make her
restless for the feel of ordinary grass on her bare feet.

CHAPTER THREE

I must look like a real princess now, she thought,
and the queen, wearing diamonds, thought so, too.
"Perhaps a bit more glitter on your lashes, dear,"
she said, "and when you dance with the prince,
remember to bend gracefully, like a willow."
But what Princess Isobel really remembered
was how, once upon a time, she and the prince
had walked among petals of white trillium
talking, always talking, their hands as warm
as the first orange ribbon of sun at dawn.
He had called her his beauty,
but now, they rarely talked at all.

CHAPTER FOUR

Like a butterfly pinned in a velvet box,
Princess Isobel sat alone, embroidering—
stitch one, loop round the needle thrice, pull through,
each glint of green thread steadying the tangle,
each knot reminding her of something round and small,
something she'd seen before. It was the pea, of course.
That stupid pea, she thought. It's not
the queen who should say if I am real or not.

So Isobel washed her face, combed out her hair,
and went to the prince in a plain-spun dress.
As he looked up from his book,
he said, "Izzy, is it really you?"

CHAPTER FIVE
His eyes were a question, his hand outstretched.
"It's *really* me," she said. "We've met before."
"Not for a chapter or two," he said, smiling,
"but we can always begin the story again."
And then, of course, she kissed him, and that was that.
No more pretending, no more glass slippers,
just the summer grass beneath their feet,
with a castle to tend, books to read,
and each other to share it all with—
two real peas in a new-fashioned pod
living their lives quite happily ever after.

The Makeover

by Bonny Becker

"You'll love the pearly glow of Sheer Magic. Try it."

Marnie leaned against her front door and stared at the smiling woman holding a bag of cosmetics samples.

"Makeup makes me break out," Marnie grumbled, mad that she'd come all the way down the stairs to answer the door for a salesperson.

"This is different," said the woman, thrusting the bottle of foundation at her.

Marnie took it and turned it in her hands. It looked just like regular old makeup to her. The bottle was small and curvy; the liquid inside was a light creamy brown. The usual. But then something shimmered under that plain surface. Something nameless and odd. Marnie blinked, and it flickered out. Must have been a trick of the light.

Makeup companies always made their stuff sound so good, she thought. They used words like *shimmer* and *sparkle* and *shine*. And she had tried them all this past year. Ever since she had started middle school and somehow it wasn't enough just to be a person anymore.

"It will make a new you," the saleswoman said.

"That would be, like, sooo great," Marnie said sarcastically. Her little laugh showed she wasn't fooled.

"Yes, it would, wouldn't it?" said the woman mildly.

Marnie looked up. Something in the woman's pale blue eyes made her swallow and say, "How much?"

"Fifty dollars."

"*What?*" Now Marnie laughed big and loud. She thrust the bottle back at the woman.

"It's a small price to pay for what you want." The woman held on to her bag with both hands, leaving Marnie still holding the foundation. "Go get the money. You have it."

The woman blinked slowly. Marnie heard the words *a new you* but the woman didn't move her lips. What would I give to be "new"? Marnie thought.

She did have exactly fifty dollars in the back of her underwear drawer upstairs.

"Go on," said the woman softly.

Marnie found herself shuffling back upstairs to get her money.

She handed it over in a hot, rolled-up cluster. The woman took it, nodded, and disappeared down the steps.

Marnie watched her go, then slumped against the wall.

What had she done? *Fifty bucks.* All the money she had!

Tears rushed to her eyes. Hot and angry. She was so sick of tears. That's all sixth grade seemed to be about—tears and crazy things like paying fifty dollars for a tiny bottle of makeup. How could she have been so stupid and so desperate!

The salespeople must know about kids like her. Kids on the edges. Staring in at the circle of popular kids who clustered in the hallway with shrieks and hugs and stories about the weekend, who gave each other balloon bouquets for birthdays and went to parties that people like her would never ever go to.

Marnie didn't know why she cared so much, but she did.

She swallowed hard. She'd been saving that money for new jeans. Something about jeans had changed; she wasn't quite sure what, but she knew that her jeans weren't right anymore and even though hers were only a month old, she needed new ones.

Marnie pushed her tears away with her palms and went to the bathroom mirror. She shook some of the foundation into her hand, then gently smoothed it across her face. She stared. Nice color. Covered up a few blotches. But her eyes were still too wide apart; her hair was still fly-away; her front teeth were still too big.

She went upstairs and shoved the makeup to the back of her drawer where her money had been.

But two days later, on Monday morning, she fished it out again and put it on. It had cost fifty dollars. She figured she might as well get something out of it.

Her best friend, Caroline, spotted her coming in the side door at school.

"Hi ya."

"Hi."

"Did you have a good weekend?"

"Ooooh, yeah, hot party," said Marnie.

Caroline smiled, but Marnie didn't. Caroline did a funny little shuffle dance to make her smile.

"Don't." Marnie blushed and looked around. She hated it when Caroline did stuff like that.

A lot of kids pretended they didn't care about being popular, but Caroline really didn't seem to. She was never going to be popular. She was heavy; her hair was thin; and she wore big, wrinkled shirts and rumpled khakis. She was also smart and funny, and even though she said pretty much what she wanted, Marnie had never seen her be mean to anyone.

Sometimes Marnie was embarrassed to be her friend, but other times when Caroline snorted at being popular, Marnie liked it. Caroline's laugh was deep and contagious. It made Marnie snicker about hair and eyeliner and nail polish and everyone crying all the time. But when Marnie cried, Caroline didn't laugh. Her kind eyes would burn with anger at the thought of anyone being mean to Marnie.

Caroline had stopped her little dance and was starting to tell Marnie about this cool role-playing Web site she had found when something astonishing happened. Something from Mars. On a cloud of perfume, someone rushed up to Marnie and grabbed her and shrieked. That someone was Heather Dixon, one of the most popular girls in school, and she was saying, "I just love your jeans. Where did you get those? Those are, like, so cool."

"I, uh, I—" Marnie could only stare.

"Did you hear what happened at Kevin's party on Saturday?"

"I, uh, I—" Nothing like real words would come out of Marnie's mouth, but it didn't matter because Heather was sweeping her along. Other kids were joining them and they were talking and laughing with Marnie right in the middle. She stared around wildly, confused. She saw Caroline on the fringes of the group; Marnie started toward her, but Amy Sutton grabbed her arm, because she just had to hear this. And what had she done to her hair? someone asked. And was she going to Aaron's bar mitzvah? It was like she had always been part of this group, the center of everything. She touched her cheek with the makeup on it.

That's what it was—the makeup. It did something. Just like that, she was popular. Marnie didn't know how or why. She didn't care. She'd just make sure she wore Sheer Magic every day.

Suddenly, kids who had always ignored her cared what she thought. If she wore something, they copied it. She was invited to all the parties. Her phone rang constantly. A dozen kids instant messaged her if she set a toe online.

It was like being a dried-up little plant and suddenly having water and sun come pouring in. She couldn't believe how good it felt to walk into school and have a dozen kids wave and say hi. To have three or four girls rush up with the latest news and have one of the cutest guys glance her way while his friends elbowed him and teased. Teased because he liked her!

"I wish my hair was wavy like yours," Heather would say, pouting.

"You have the prettiest smile," Amy would add with an envious sigh.

"Guess who likes you?" Jennifer would whisper, pulling her aside.

Just like the saleswoman had said. It made her new. People saw her differently now. They had forgotten all about the old her.

Except for Caroline. At first Caroline had looked puzzled, but when she tried to talk to Marnie about it, laughing about how weird it was, Marnie had shrugged.

"They're not so bad when you get to know them," she said.

"Well, if you don't mind comparing lip gloss all day," said Caroline, rumbling with her deep laugh.

But Marnie didn't join in.

"You wouldn't understand," she said, and she walked away with a hard little twitch to her shoulders.

She started avoiding Caroline, walking quickly past her in the mornings by the side door, pretending not to see her at lunch, not meeting her eye.

It was easy to stay away from Caroline because these days Marnie was always surrounded by her many new friends, all eager for her attention and approval. She was so popular that one day she didn't bother with Sheer Magic. She didn't need it anymore. She put on the Shimmering Champagne she and Heather had found at the mall that weekend.

At the side door, she waved as Heather and Jennifer came rushing in. She said with a smirk, "Did you hear what Kevin did to Tracey?"

Heather and Jennifer stared at her like they'd never seen her before.

"Excuse me?" said Heather, like Marnie was something on her shoe. "Are you talking to me?"

"Like, duh," said Marnie. "What's the problem?"

"Do we know her?" Jennifer said to Heather.

"I hope not," said Heather.

"Heather! Come on," said Marnie, trying to laugh as if it were a joke, but she knew it wasn't. She just didn't want to believe it was only the makeup and nothing more. She grabbed at Heather's arm.

"Hey, don't touch!" Heather cried, repulsed.

"Leave us alone, whoever you are," said Jennifer. She turned away, then turned back. "By the way, I hate to tell you, but that stuff you've got on your face? Whatever it is, it doesn't hide UGLY."

She and Heather laughed and swept into the school.

Marnie sat down on the steps and, with trembling fingers, smeared on Sheer Magic.

"Hey, Marnie, wait up for me!" Kevin yelled from the parking lot.

"So that's how you do it," said Caroline.

Marnie glanced up. Caroline stood at the foot of the steps. She'd seen it all.

"Want some?" Marnie asked softly.

"No way." Caroline shook her head and walked on by.

Even though Caroline was big, she had a stately way of walking. Sometimes Marnie thought of her as a kind of queen. A skinny girl with acne who got teased a lot came up beside Caroline and said something with a shy, anxious smile. Caroline smiled back, laughing her deep ocean laugh.

Marnie suddenly wanted to know what the girl had said. She wanted to laugh with them, but just then Kevin caught up with her and began bragging about how wild he'd been at the party on Saturday.

Marnie began to notice how she didn't have to avoid Caroline anymore. Caroline wasn't paying any attention. She was there as she had always been—on the edges—but now she talked with other kids, not Marnie. They looked like they were having fun. Marnie wanted to push over there and find out what they were talking about, but there were so many people in her way now.

Several times, Marnie thought she should call Caroline, but then remembered how Caroline had ignored her and then she didn't have the nerve.

Then one morning Marnie pushed open the door to the girls' bathroom and saw that Caroline was in there alone.

"Hi," said Marnie softly.

Caroline looked up. She didn't say anything.

Marnie blushed.

"I'm sorry," she said. "I don't know why I've been acting this way. Or, I mean, I do know, but I . . ."

Marnie's voice trailed off. What could she say?

"I guess I don't really blame you," Caroline suddenly said. "It would be pretty hard to resist being so popular."

Marnie nodded, glancing shyly at her old friend.

"But doesn't it bother you that it's not real?" said Caroline. "It's not about you at all."

"Nobody's popular for any real reason," said Marnie. "I mean, so what? I mean the point is just to be popular . . . isn't it?"

"Hmmmm." Caroline didn't really argue, but she didn't look impressed.

Marnie fumbled in her book bag and held out the bottle of Sheer Magic.

"Come on," she said. "Try it. Please?"

Caroline shook her head.

"Why not?" cried Marnie.

It would be so easy if Caroline would. It would be so perfect! Caroline shrugged. "I don't know. It's just not me, I guess."

Caroline suddenly grinned and did her little shuffle dance. "I gotta be me," she sang out in a phony Broadway musical kind of way.

Just then Heather and a group of girls swept in. Marnie was surrounded, engulfed in their chatter as they fussed in front of the mirror. Caroline was shoved to one side.

Heather glanced at Caroline, then leaned toward Marnie, saying in a deliberately loud voice, "I wonder why fat people think those big, sloppy shirts hide anything."

Then she shuddered. "Like, ick!"

Jennifer squealed with laughter and shuddered, too. As if Caroline was a gross bug, a snake, a worm.

Marnie blinked, then looked straight at Caroline and said to her, "Watch this."

She grabbed a paper towel and carefully wiped off all the Sheer Magic.

And it *was* magic how the girls turned away and dropped their eager efforts to get Marnie's attention. They didn't even seem to know that they had been talking to her.

Marnie quickly dabbed on a bit of Sheer Magic. The girls turned back and the squeals immediately rose up around her.

Marnie wiped it off and she was nothing.

She dabbed it on and she was the center.

Off. On. Cold. Hot. Popular. Not. The girls were like machines she could control. Marnie did it faster and faster. Frowns, smiles. Silence, squeals. Like a weird, speeded-up cartoon. And suddenly it was so silly that Caroline began to laugh. An ocean of a laugh, a laugh Marnie hadn't heard in a long time. A laugh so big it seemed to lift Marnie up with it. Up to where she could see.

And she saw that someday it wouldn't matter. Someday even Heather and Jennifer wouldn't care about being popular. Someday they would all wonder why they had thought it was so important.

She began to laugh, too. Loud and hard. She turned toward Caroline. Caroline, who had never not seen her, the real her, and was still her friend.

Heather and Jennifer and the others didn't know what the laughing was about, and they glanced anxiously at each other. Heather twitched her shoulders. She looked like she wanted to say something mean, but the words wouldn't come out. She swallowed and hastily patted on some blush.

Marnie reached up and felt her cheek. She would miss it, she supposed. "Someday" wasn't here yet. Later today or tomorrow or the next day, she might miss not being in the center of squeals and gossip, but that wouldn't last. It would be okay.

She held the little bottle of Sheer Magic in her hand and studied it. Then, as she and Caroline headed out the door of the girls' bathroom, she tossed it in the trash.

Girlfriends

by Sara Holbrook

Such a private

conversation

that words would interfere.

We reach out and

grasp

what no one else can hear.

An arm around the waist,

a hug

or slight of hand.

The eloquence of touch—

a language

only girlfriends

understand.

Where the Lilacs Grow

by Pamela Smith Hill

Sister Paris's roses smelled like poison. My nose was just inches away from an orange Tropicana as big as Kenny Royal's fist, and all I could smell were chemicals. Not even a whiff of tea rose. Nana's roses had always smelled like *roses*—all luscious and sweet, almost ticklish. They'd grown in curved rows along the south side of the house, where the sunshine warmed away the dew and dried up the black spot that ate away at Sister Paris's roses. I stripped off a whole stem of spotty yellow and black leaves. It dropped into my basket along with all the rest.

"Rose on a stick, that's what she grows," Nana had said in April when I told her I'd be working at Sister Paris's three afternoons a week. "Be sure to wear gloves, Lorena. And throw your work clothes down the laundry shoot the minute you're finished. Heaven knows, she smothers those bushes of hers with rose dust."

Nana hadn't known then that our new house wouldn't have a laundry shoot, but she was right about the rose dust.

"Are you finished yet, Lorena?" Sister Paris tottered out through the garage and into the north shade, where most of her roses grew. Tropicanas, Mr. Lincolns, Elizabeth Ardens, and a whole bunch I didn't recognize by name. They were lined up in rows alongside the driveway.

"Yes, ma'am," I said, dropping one last handful of sickly stems into the basket.

She shook her head and frowned. "Have you ever seen such a pathetic sight?"

Well, at least she was honest.

Orange, red, pink, yellow, and white puffs of color burst into flower at the end of dozens of bare branches. She sighed and folded her skinny, old-lady arms across her chest. "Manure. That was your grandmother's secret. She'd have your dad pile up a seasoned supply in April, and by June, her roses were the marvel of all the ladies at both churches—the Bolivar and Bona congregations combined. Never did have to spray a single leaf."

Which was true, of course.

The manure helped, but so did all that hot, south, summer sunshine. Of an August afternoon like this one, Nana's roses would be blooming like the sparkles on a rhinestone bracelet. Our white lace curtains at the dining-room windows would stir in the breeze. A cardinal might call from the dogwoods down toward the kitchen, and the smell of fresh-mown hay would come drifting up from the pasture.

Home.

But home was gone—or all that truly made it home.

"Did your folks save your grandmother's lilacs?" Sister Paris asked, taking the basket of sick leaves from my hands. "To my way of thinking, they were even more precious than the roses."

I took off my gloves, working my hands out carefully to keep from touching too much poison. All the while, I was thinking about the lilacs, how they'd looked that first week in May—

seven great, towering columns of deep, dark purple; soft, airy lavender; and lacy white. They'd bloomed like heaven, as if they knew the end was near—the Royals' big jack coming to wrench the house from its foundation and rip their roots right out of the ground. And then water. Tons and tons of water. Unimaginable water, which would cover everything by this time next year. . . .

"The lilacs, Lorena," said Sister Paris, clearing her throat. "Did your folks save the lilac bushes?"

I shook my head, remembering the heaps of flowering branches Nana and I had gathered during those final weeks—lilacs for the dining-room table, the piano in the living room, the oak cupboard in the kitchen. "The pure smell of springtime," Nana had said. Finally all alone, I'd picked one last bouquet—for Nana's bedside.

"They're all gone, then?"

I stared up at the sky, not wanting to look Sister Paris in the face for fear I'd start to cry. At last I said, "Kenny Royal and his brothers ripped most of them out when they moved the house. All that's left are the two white ones by the front porch."

Sister Paris shook her head and mumbled, "The whole country's gone dam crazy."

Dam—as in Stockton Dam. For Sister Paris would never utter a true swear word, nor would any of my parents' friends at either church—the one at Bona or the one in Bolivar. But even the ladies used that phrase now.

Dam crazy.

I'd probably heard it every day for the last four years, starting with the first time—in Humbert's Store after Sunday services at the Bona church. I'd walked across the highway to get my little sisters some cherry-flavored Life Savers. Kenny Royal was buying a pack of Camels, which he always smoked privately in his pickup truck after church.

"The whole country's gone dam crazy," he was saying to Mr. Humbert. "The Clarks, Tedricks, and Whites are gonna lose their farms. Saw it yesterday on a Corps of Engineers map over in Stockton. I hear the Wildman place will be under water, too."

Under water . . .

Our house—the Wildman place.

I'd hurried out the swinging glass door and completely forgot to pay for those Life Savers. But I have a feeling Mr. Humbert wouldn't have charged me anyway, not then, not when he knew such news would plain cut through my heart.

"Well, it's a mercy your grandmother didn't live to see the day," Sister Paris was saying. "Sometimes I wish I hadn't lived to see this day myself, folks feeling so unsettled, losing their farms." Her eyes squinted up into wrinkles. "It don't matter one bit that the government finally paid y'all for the land. You had no choice in the matter. Nobody did."

"That's what everybody says," I replied, remembering the handshakes at the funeral, the notes scribbled across the bottom of sympathy cards. I wished Sister Paris would stop all this talk and let me go home.

Finally she dropped four quarters in my hand and sighed. "You do good work, Lorena," she said. "Your grandmother would have been proud."

I nodded and slipped the quarters, three days' pay, into my pocket and started down the driveway. But Sister Paris called me back.

"Are you and your folks driving over to the Bona house tonight?" she asked.

"Yes, ma'am. One last trip before school starts back up again."
I thought of the bare, empty house waiting for us tonight, just
sitting there on what the Corps of Engineers called "high ground."
Why did we have to go back? The house looked so sad and
lonely, perched there in the middle of a torn-up alfalfa field.

Sister Paris touched my shoulder. "Take some of these along
with you." She snipped off three Tropicanas-on-a-stick, blew on
the flowers to get some of the rose dust off, then held them out
for me. "Your grandmother always kept a bouquet of flowers on
her dining-room table."

"That's very kind of you." I took the roses but didn't tell
her that Nana's dining-room table had been sold at auction. It
was too big for the house in Bolivar we'd moved into last
month.

Just as I reached the street, Sister Paris's quavery voice called
out, "Think about those lilac bushes, Lorena. They're worth
saving."

A gospel-meeting sign was taped to the window of Dad's barbershop, and I bent close to read it:

BONA GOSPEL MEETING
With Brother *Eddie Stanton*
Minister of the Church of Christ, Bolivar, Missouri
Gather to hear the soul-stirring Word of God at

BONA COMMUNITY CHURCH
SEPTEMBER 26–OCTOBER 2, 1969

"Go ye into all the world and preach the Gospel"

Strange that the preacher from our new church would soon be preaching at our old one. But then Nana had once said that the folks at the Bolivar congregation were almost like family. That's why Mom and Dad had decided to move here once they were sure that Stockton Lake would flood all but fourteen acres of the farm. That and the fact that Dad's barbershop had been in Bolivar ever since I could remember.

"Hi, Lorena," he called through the open door. "How did things go over at Sister Paris's?" His scissors skimmed over the top of Dr. Buzard's thinning hair.

"Just fine," I said, taking in the clean, spicy smell of shampoo and aftershave. For a moment, I could almost forget the stink of poison rising off those roses.

"When's Sister Paris gonna learn that you can't grow roses along the north side of a house?" Dad asked, nodding at my sickly bouquet.

"Careful there, Loren." Dr. Buzard grinned at Dad. "Sickly as those things are, they're Elmira Paris's pride and joy."

"She wants us to take them with us tonight—to Bona, I mean." I paused, not knowing what else to say, not wanting to remind Dad of the glorious summertime bouquets that used to fill every room when Nana was alive. It was like the house had died with her—those bare windows and nothing inside but sleeping cots, an old card table, a camp stove, and boxes of junk that hadn't sold at auction. The house didn't even have electricity or real plumbing anymore.

Dad set his shears aside and reached for the clippers. "That's mighty kind of Sister Paris. Why don't you set those roses in some water until I'm finished here."

I walked to the back of the shop, found an empty glass, and filled it with water. Dad and Dr. Buzard were talking politics. Dad supported President Nixon's policies in Vietnam; Dr. Buzard, who taught English at the Baptist Bible College, did not. I didn't know what to believe.

I set the glass of roses in the back-room windowsill, then rinsed the rose dust from my hands. Rex Heatherly from the Bona church had been killed in Vietnam; nobody was sure just how—and maybe we didn't really want to know. Nana, Mom, and I had served cake in the church basement for his funeral. A year before that, the three of us had stood in exactly the same spot, serving up wedding cake when he'd married Arlene Martin.

"Such a tragedy," Nana had said, glancing over at Arlene, all dressed in black for the funeral. "A young man shot down before he's had a chance to live, to know what's important in this life and what isn't. Me, on the other hand, I've had a good long life—and enjoyed nearly every minute of it. I want you both to remember that, come what may."

Then my eyes had filled with sudden tears. Not for Rex or Arlene Heatherly—but for Nana. We'd all just learned that her cancer had come back and the doctors said there was nothing more they could do for her.

"Lorena," Dad called, "you can walk on home if you want to. I'm going to be here a while longer."

I dried my hands and leaned against the doorway. Dr. Buzard held a mirror in his hand and was scowling at his reflection. Despite the fact that he didn't have a full head of hair, he had always been one of Dad's most demanding customers.

"Or," Dad said, smiling, "you could run over to the Rexall for a cherry Coke and we could walk home together." He fished a dime out of his pocket. "I'll buy."

I drifted over to the soda fountain counter, which was empty, and waited to order my cherry Coke. Nana, of course, would have walked right across the store to the cosmetics department, where a girl not much older than me was reading a *Seventeen* magazine. "I need some help at the soda fountain, please," Nana would have said. But I couldn't imagine myself ever doing *that*. Finally, the girl looked up.

"Oh, I'm sorry," she said. She tucked the *Seventeen* under her arm and walked across the store, past the Ace bandages and flashlight batteries. "Have you seen these new maxi skirts?" she asked, opening the magazine to pictures of girls wearing old-fashioned-looking skirts that went all the way to their ankles. "I can't believe my luck," she went on. "I finally get my mom used to miniskirts and now this!"

I just nodded. Who cared, really? Maxiskirts, miniskirts. It just didn't interest me.

She closed the magazine and smiled. "What'll you have?"

I was almost embarrassed to order. It seemed kind of imma-ture to ask for a cherry Coke, but I'd never ordered anything else at the Rexall fountain. Then, just when I'd decided on a Dr Pep-per, the girl said, "I'm going to make myself a cherry Coke. Mr. Lowry lets me have one a day—on the house."

I smiled back. "I'll have the same."

Nobody but the pharmacist was in the store, so we took our cherry Cokes back across to the cosmetic counter, where a whole row of glass shelves was filled with bright boxes of perfume and powder. Revolving racks held Revlon lipsticks, Maybelline mascaras, and Max Factor eye shadows. I recognized one of Nana's favorites—Charles of the Ritz loose powder, in a round, gold-trimmed box. Mom didn't approve of makeup. But Nana did.

"Lorena's old enough for a little lipstick and powder, don't you think, Lillian?" Nana had said. "She'll be driving before you know it."

Mom shook her head. "She won't need lipstick to drive a car."

It was one of the few things they'd quarreled about.

A display of clear, rosy containers caught my eye—Bloom rouge. Nana used to dab a little on her index and middle fingers, then lightly tap it onto her cheeks.

"Oh, you don't want that," the girl said, tossing her hair, which was long and blond and perfectly straight. "Look at this." She pointed to a bright display on top of the counter. "Bonne Bell lip gloss. Real natural. Want to try some?" She held out a sample, along with a mirror.

I dipped my finger into a little pot of goo and wiped it across my lips. Just a tint of pink, which looked surprisingly nice. I checked the price—ninety-nine cents, a week of work at Sister Paris's. I looked back at my reflection and smiled. It might be worth it.

Then all of a sudden the girl sprayed me with perfume. It gave off the vague scent of lilacs, sweet and clean, like springtime itself. And somehow, it was like I was back at the farm, clipping lilacs with Nana, filling our baskets with pale lavender, white, and deep purple spikes of flowers. We were walking slow around the house, talking about the future.

My future.

"You mustn't be afraid of what's ahead, Lorena," she was saying. "High school, college. Follow in your mother's footsteps. Get all the education you can."

By then, we'd stopped by the front porch and she was clipping whole branches of heavy white lilacs. "I'm proud of your dad, proud of what he and your Fafa did with this farm—not to mention that your dad's the best barber in southwest Missouri. But times are changing. Don't dwell on things done and gone."

The girl sprayed me again, then sprayed herself. "Rub your wrists together like this," she said. "See? To make the perfume last."

Dad was locking up, Sister Paris's Tropicanas in one hand, his keys in the other. "You smell real good, Lorena," he said. "Better than the poison on these roses, that's for sure."

We walked past the Tastee Freeze, where a line was already beginning to form, then farther down—past the Pitts Funeral Chapel, the Good Samaritan Old Folks Home, and the Butler Funeral Home. A steady stream of Saturday night traffic cruised by, cars filled mostly with students from the Baptist Bible College; they'd go down to the end of Hartford Street, then turn around and start the whole circle all over again. A couple of cars honked and Dad waved back. It took us all of five minutes to get home.

Home.

But it didn't feel like home—a low, squat, stucco house in town with a wide front porch stretching from one end to the other; the TV news pouring out of the screen door onto the porch; Mom's lesson plans for next week spread across the ugly new dining-room table.

Our old table, the one sold at auction, had been graceful and wide—wide enough to spread out all those Corps of Engineers maps the government man brought with him when he visited us that first time. Dad's hands had trembled when the man had pointed to the big blue patch right in the center—the lake that would swallow everything up so folks in Springfield could turn on a light switch or run their air conditioners.

"You have no choice, son," Nana had said then, steadying Dad's hands. "But the house. Seems to me you could move it there—to the east and south." She'd pointed to that little scrap of property the lake wouldn't take.

But that hadn't really saved the house for us.

Not for *us*.

Because this time next year, somebody else would be living there. Mom and Dad had decided to rent out the house and start a college fund for me and my sisters with the rent money.

"It's the right thing to do, Lorena," Nana had said when I took her that last bunch of lilacs. "Taking the government money for the farm and buying a house in Bolivar—you'll get a better education there. It's a college town." This last she'd said in that no-nonsense voice of hers. When she talked like that, even Mom couldn't argue with her.

So there we were, in a house that wasn't home—my little sisters, Lenna and Laura, arguing about which one would be Miss Scarlet in a game of Clue, and Mom in the kitchen making bologna sandwiches. "Lorena," she called, "would you take that pile of dirty clothes down to the basement for me?"

A house with no laundry chute.

A house without rose bushes. Without lilacs. Without Nana.

We ate our bologna sandwiches, folded up the laundry, and

packed up our pajamas and Sunday clothes. Finally, around seven o'clock we all piled into the car and headed toward Bona. Mom and Dad still called it home. But nothing felt like home to me anymore.

After services at the Bona church that next morning, we ate lunch at Brother and Sister Young's. They were *old* newlyweds, married not a year ago. What I mean is that they both had grown children, gray hair, and faces lined with wrinkles. But everybody I knew loved to talk about their courtship. She had been widowed for ever so long, and so had he. Finally, they'd met about two years ago at a gospel meeting, while she was visiting a cousin who lived by the Royals. Brother Young asked her over for pie and ice cream after every service. He baked the pie himself. Finally he popped the question and she said yes. Now they lived in his big white house, just below the Bona Church. The Stockton Lake wouldn't swallow up any of their property.

"Imogene Young is living life the right way," Nana had said after she heard about the match. "But I wouldn't trade places with her for all the world—not after living life with your Fafa. I had him for fifty years, but that wasn't long enough."

That wasn't long enough.

That's what I was thinking about, standing all alone in the house—Nana's house, our house, our shell of a house. Mom, Dad, Lenna, and Laura had gone down to the swimming hole for the afternoon, but I'd preferred to stay behind, roaming through every room, remembering.

Remembering Christmases and birthdays, falls and springs, Sunday afternoons—almost like this one, with Nana and Fafa napping upstairs, Mom grading papers, Dad and my sisters whooping it up outside somewhere. I'd be left to myself—to read a book, take a walk, or just sit in the porch swing, thinking.

Now the house was so bare and empty and sad. Blank, bright squares of color, where pictures had once hung, stared back at me from faded walls. Sister Paris's Tropicanas drooped out of a mason jar on the floor. Then there were those great cracks, new cracks, which ran from floor to ceiling, formed when the Royal brothers had jacked up the house with their special machinery and lifted it whole onto a flatbed trailer. The Boliver *Free Press* and the *Cedar County Republican* had run pictures of our house on the front page with great big headlines:

WILDMAN HOMESTEAD SEEKS HIGHER GROUND
TWO-STORY FARMHOUSE CREEPS UP HIGHWAY 245

Mom had cut out the stories and pasted them into her scrapbook, alongside Nana's obituary, which had appeared in both papers not two weeks earlier.

I wandered upstairs and stood looking out the window in Nana's bedroom. Far away, I could almost make out the line of hills where the Sac River would soon be dammed, sending water out over thousands of acres. I thought of the abandoned farms, the hundreds of families who couldn't afford to save their houses or didn't have land nearby that could shelter them. I tried, tried, tried to feel lucky.

But I couldn't.

I turned away—and that's when I saw it. A cardboard box peeping out of Nana's closet. I pulled the box out. It contained Nana's gardening clothes—a pair of faded denim pants, two old denim shirts, canvas shoes without the shoestrings, her lopsided straw hat, and a pair of rhinestone earrings—and at the very bottom, her favorite pruning shears and a book—*The Gardener's Companion.*

I clipped on the earrings, took the book downstairs, and sat crosslegged in front of Sister Paris's Tropicanas. Sure enough, here were all the things Nana had always told me about roses:

1. Plant them in direct sun, preferably in a south-facing bed.
2. Water only in the morning on dry, sunny days.
3. Fertilize rose beds with seasoned manure in the early spring.
4. Pick off diseased leaves by hand and discard them away from your roses.

But there was more, a lot more—about planning out flower-beds, choosing the right plants for a garden, and taking cuttings from hearty plants.

Did your folks save the lilacs?

Shadows began to creep across the living-room floor. Lenna and Laura's voices called to me from the field just beyond the barbed wire fence. But I didn't call back. I raced upstairs, squashed Nana's hat on my head, grabbed up her pruning shears, then ran outside—through the Royals' truck ruts, past the alfalfa field and across the highway. Sweat beaded up under my bangs, trickled down my chest, dampened the armholes under my blouse. Pickup trucks, sedans, and station wagons went roaring past. Finally, I reached the cutoff to our old road, where our house used to sit.

Just past the little dip in the road, I turned off and walked up our old driveway. A cool breeze rustled through the oaks and dogwoods, still there, spreading their leaves over the broken rubble of our old foundation. Deep ruts scarred the lawn. Dandelion puffs scattered in the wind. But there they were—Nana's two white lilacs, robust and healthy, standing like guardians before what had once been the front porch.

I closed my eyes and remembered all that I'd known before— the house standing tall against the oaks and the dogwoods, its lace curtains fluttering in the breeze, Nana moving slow and sure among the lilacs, a basket of flowers on her arm. I ran my fingers over a branch of lilac and remembered their fragrance, the brilliance of their bright white against a cloudy day.

Then I reached for Nana's pruning shears and took first one cutting and then another and another. If I tended them well, they just might take root in new soil, at a new home.

It was up to me.

This Is the Way It Is

by Miriam Bat-Ami

This is the way it is with me and my horse,
not at all like school
where mostly I am silent
even when I know the answers.
No one wants to be a brainiac.

I squeeze slightly with the insides of my calves
near the bottom of her barrel.
She asks, "What?" I say, "Now."

My horse doesn't care about the tear in my jacket
or my stained pants. She doesn't care
about my hair or think that I'm too smart
for my own good.
Her ears ask. I answer.

This is the way it is with my horse and me,
not like school at all.
I don't have to close my mouth
or make my arms stay close to my sides
when they'd rather be
students of the sky, saying,
"I know that one. I knew it last year." I said that in class,

and Greg (who is handsome as a horse
except his nose is shorter)
shook his head and made a funny face so his friends laughed.
    "She's a brainiac.
    She's a nerd.
    She's one of those suck-up girls."

I wish the barn were the world.

My teacher at the barn is fifty-five.
Her face is cracked in all the used places
like worn leather boots that still shine when you polish them.
Her hands remind me of underground vegetables:
radishes and turnips and rutabaga.
They're hard and strong and rough and red
and they always feel soft
on a horse's mouth.

"You have to know where you're going," my teacher says.
"If you don't, the horse will decide for you."
I have to become head of a herd of two,
but sometimes that's hard. Today
it's even harder.

In science class our teacher asked,
"What is the process called when leaves use sunlight
to make food?"

Way back in third grade I made a map
with a tree and green leaves

and the sun and the soil.
I labeled everything with a green pencil
because green is for growing.
"Photosynthesis," I wrote.
Way back in third grade
I was the sun and the tree and the leaves
working on green.

My science teacher looked at me.
He sometimes forgets and thinks I'm the old me,
the brainiac.
I looked back at him with my dumb look,
not dumb dumb
just sort of dumb
like you could almost get the answer
if you really tried.

I made my face look blank
and my eyes look even blanker.
I forced my arms to stay at my sides,
and I felt sad inside like something had shrunk
to the size of a prune.

I wish the barn were the world.

The Secret Behind the Stone

by Sandy Asher

"Who is *that?*"

"Where'd she get the dress?"

"Little early for Halloween, isn't it?"

"All she needs is a broom."

Mrs. Cooper rapped her knuckles on her desktop. "Settle down, fifth graders."

The room stopped buzzing. But eyes went on rolling. And snickerers went on snickering, hands pressed tight over their mouths. The new girl couldn't have missed the warm welcome.

I know all about being the new girl. In the last five years, I've been the new girl three times. My mom went back to school when my little brother, Davey, started first grade. That was our first move, closer to the university. She'd already graduated college before she and Dad got divorced, but she wanted a master's degree in business administration.

"Takes an MBA to make a CEO," she says. A CEO is a Chief Executive Officer—the person who runs a big corporation and makes tons of money. We could use tons of money, since Dad didn't leave much when he skipped out. So now Mom's "climbing the corporate ladder," and every rung seems to be in a different state.

This year, we're in St. Louis, Missouri. It's fine. Pretty house, great zoo, lots of museums and malls and other cool stuff.

School's okay, too. I like Mrs. Cooper. I get along as best I can with everybody who's willing to get along with me, and I don't worry about the creeps. I don't have time! There's no telling when Mom'll come bouncing into the house after work with that "I got another promotion" grin on her face and we'll be packing up again. So I don't knock myself out to make friends. Not close friends, anyway.

I certainly wasn't expecting to get close to Tracy Anderson. But when she showed up in our classroom with that panicky new girl look in her eyes, my heart went out to her. At least I'd started the new school at the beginning of the year. Here it was October: Everybody knew everybody else, and we all knew the routine. She was two months behind and a total stranger.

"Yes, dear?"

Mrs. Cooper smiled, and Tracy shuffled over to the desk in sneakers that didn't seem to fit any better than her saggy green dress. She handed over a large white card.

"Oh, so you're Tracy Anderson!" Mrs. Cooper said, her dark eyes sparkling over her reading glasses. "I've been expecting you. Welcome!

"Class, this is Tracy Anderson. She's just moved to St. Louis from . . ." Mrs. Cooper glanced over at Tracy, waiting for her to fill in the blank. Tracy's eyes grew wider and even more alarmed. Realizing she'd made a bad move, Mrs. Cooper quickly consulted the white card in her hand. "Tracy's just moved here from

Sikeston," she announced. "I expect you all to make her feel welcome and help her find her way around."

The bell rang just then; time for us to go to Music. People scraped back their chairs, stood up, and started talking; but Mrs. Cooper rapped the desk again and waited, frowning, until we were all back in our seats and quiet.

"I decide when you're dismissed," she reminded us, "not the bell. I would like someone to walk Tracy downstairs to the music room."

My hand shot into the air. I don't know why. There was just something about Tracy Anderson that called out to me. New-girl sympathy, I guess.

"Lindsay!" Mrs. Cooper's pleased smile made me feel I'd definitely made the right choice. "Thank you, dear. Tracy, this is Lindsay Federow. She'll take good care of you."

If Tracy believed that, she didn't show it. She watched me move up the aisle toward her without cracking a smile—or changing her expression in any way at all. Either she just didn't care—or she was frozen in place, like a rabbit.

"Gonna go trick or treating?" Mitchell Stevens whispered as I passed his desk. I ignored him—and the giggles from those nearby who'd heard him.

"Hi," I said to Tracy.

She nodded. At least, I think she did. It was that small.

The crowd at the door actually made way for us, stepping back and gawking as if we were some sort of float in a parade.

"This way." I guided Tracy to the left and down the stairs toward the music room. "Have you seen much of St. Louis yet?" I asked.

No answer.

I babbled on for a while about moving to St. Louis and then switched to filling her in on Mr. Everett's music class and how the class creeps spent all their time purposely singing off-key to drive him crazy.

"Funny thing about creeps," I found myself telling her, "everywhere you go, there's another batch. And they're all the same. They pretend they're better than everyone else and they tease you and try to make you feel bad. But if you don't care— or don't show them you care—they back off. I guess it's just no fun for them if you don't react. That's Mr. Everett's problem: He reacts—big time! His face gets all purple and he yells and snaps his batons in two! They love that. It makes their day."

As if to prove my point, Mitchell and two of his buddies sidled up to us outside the music room. "Is Witchy-poo going to sing us a little solo?" he asked.

Ignoring him as usual, I turned toward Tracy—who looked pretty close to fainting. I'd read about skin turning "ashen" before, but I'd never actually seen it.

"Maybe she's a baritone," Mitchell went on. "Or a bass!"

His friends thought that was so hilarious, they had to prop themselves against the wall to keep from toppling over with laughter.

I hurried Tracy into the music room. But Mitchell was right: She would be asked to sing by herself—unless she could tell Mr. Everett whether she was a soprano or alto.

That's when I got my first brilliant idea: If she was too shy to talk, maybe she could write! I had her sit in a chair next to mine. Mr. Everett was busy listing musical terms on the board: *allegro, andante* . . .

I tore a piece of paper out of my notebook. "Soprano or alto?" I scribbled and passed the note and my pencil across the aisle.

Tracy looked at the paper and then at me. Her eyes were very pale blue—and not quite so frightened. She underlined soprano twice and passed back the note and pencil. I grinned at her and wrote, "Me, too."

She took the paper and pencil again. "I'm glad," she wrote— and grinned back.

The instant Mr. Everett turned around, I had my hand in the air. "This is Tracy Anderson," I informed him. "She's new in our class, and she's a soprano. Like me. Mrs. Cooper asked me to help her out."

Mr. Everett eyed Tracy from under his bushy brows for about half a second. "Fine. Thank you—um—"

"Lindsay," I reminded him.

He ran a freckled hand through the long wisps of white hair that didn't come close to covering his bald spot. "Yes, of course. Thank you, Lindsay."

"No problem, Mr. Everett."

Mitchell swiveled around in his tenor section seat and made kissing noises in my direction.

At about the same time, Tracy wrote "Thanks!" and smiled again as she passed me the message.

"You're welcome," I wrote back. Mitchell was still waiting for my reaction, so I blew him a kiss. He turned away, blushing.

And Tracy giggled!

She had a great giggle—tinkly and sweet, like the wind chime on our next-door neighbor's back porch. It was the kind of giggle that made you want to hear it again.

That was the beginning of our friendship—and our note-writing.

It was weird. We quickly became inseparable at school—sitting side by side in our classes and at lunch, working on the same committees, volunteering for library duty together. And we talked, finally, but only about stuff going on at school. She didn't seem comfortable talking about anything else—hobbies, pets, movies she'd been to, trips to the mall, not even her favorite TV shows. All I knew for sure about her family was that she had a mother, a stepdad, and a much older sister who didn't live at home anymore. Tracy's clothes were mostly her sister's hand-me-downs.

Maybe I should have realized right off that something was wrong, but I didn't. Whenever she didn't want to talk, she'd kind of duck her head and look so uneasy, I'd back off. I kept thinking I was the one with the problem, asking questions that embarrassed her like that.

"Invite her over for dinner," Mom suggested more than once. "I'll be glad to drive her home if her parents can't pick her up. Or ask her to spend the night."

But no matter how many times I asked, Tracy wouldn't come to my house, not even for a couple of hours after school, and she never explained why. "I just can't" was all she said.

She seemed so miserable about saying it that I finally stopped asking.

She never invited me to her house, either. Or called me on the phone. And the one time I tried calling her, she said she couldn't talk. She practically hung up on me! I thought maybe she'd been grounded, although it was hard to imagine Tracy in trouble. At school the next day, she told me her stepdad didn't want the phone tied up, so please don't call again.

It seemed very hard for her to say that. She looked . . . scared. Did she think I was angry at her? "It's okay," I said. "Parents can be so weird sometimes." She nodded at that and smiled at me. It felt good to make her smile.

We didn't see or talk to one another at all on weekends. And the strangest thing was that she always seemed quieter on Mondays. Not that she was ever exactly noisy, but it was almost as if we had to start the whole friendship over every week.

On our last day of school before winter break, we were walking home in even more silence than usual. Tracy had made it clear that she didn't want to talk about her family's plans for the holidays, and I'd run out of ways to get any other conversation going. I was starting to feel every bit as gray and gloomy as the afternoon sky when I noticed a new "for sale" sign in a lot at the corner where Tracy turned east and I turned west. The restaurant that used to be there had been totally gutted by a kitchen fire. All that was left of it now was a small hill of rocks and rubble piled up against the wall of the building next door.

That's when I got my second brilliant idea. "You know what we could do?" I said. "We could leave each other notes over the holiday. Not every day, maybe, but whenever we get the chance."

Tracy brightened a little. "We could?" she asked.

"Sure!" I searched around the rubble and pulled away the largest stone I could find. "We'll hide them right behind here."

"What if somebody else finds them?"

"Who would know to look? Besides, we don't have to use our names. I'll know it's you and you'll know it's me."

Tracy frowned for a moment. "I won't be able to do it every day."

"That's okay. Whenever we're out, running errands or whatever, we can just check behind the stone. If there's a note, fine. If not, well, maybe next time. It'll be fun!"

Tracy giggled.

"Okay?" I asked.

"Okay," she said.

"Okay!" I was glad to hear her laugh as we went our separate ways. "Have a happy holiday!" I called after her. She waved one mittened hand without turning around.

I left my first note the very next morning:

Hi!

My mom, Davey, and I went to the mall last night, and we got in line at Santa's Toyland so Davey could talk to Santa. He was all excited about it until he was sitting in Santa's lap. One up-close "ho-ho-ho" and he burst into tears! Mom had to dash up there and rescue him. The photographer took a picture of Davey bawling, which Mom had to buy, of course.

That wasn't the worst thing that happened, though. While Mom was paying the photographer, another kid peed in Santa's lap!

I don't think his mom bought that photo!

XOXO,

Me

I could just imagine Tracy giggling when she read my note and couldn't wait to read what she wrote back.

I had a long wait. I checked behind the stone every day of

winter break. I love to get mail! But I didn't get anything from Tracy for nearly a week. I just kept finding my own notes, still waiting to be picked up. And each time, I added another to the pile. I told her about seeing *The Nutcracker* ballet with Mom and about the video games I got from my dad—so babyish I gave them to Davey.

> *What I really wish he'd give me is a puppy. But he's probably asked Mom about that, and it's a no-no. "We move around too much," she says. "It wouldn't be fair to a dog."*
>
> *Maybe I should ask for a hamster. Maybe I could train it to walk on a leash! And shake hands! And roll over! And speak!*
>
> *It wouldn't really be the same, though, would it?*
>
> *XOXO,*
> *Me, again*

When I finally got a note from Tracy—at last!—it seemed as exciting as discovering buried treasure. It was written on a torn scrap of notebook paper:

> *Hi—*
> *I'm sorry I couldn't pick up your notes and write back sooner. I've been kind of sick. My mom and stepdad wouldn't let me go out.*
>
> *I liked your story about Davey and that kid who peed on Santa Claus! But your trained hamster was even funnier!*
>
> *I wish I had a dog, too. Or a hamster. Even a little brother would be fun.*
>
> *I wish you were my sister.*
> *XOXO*

There was just enough time for me to write once more after that, to tell her I was glad she liked my stories and hoped she was feeling better.

We can be pretend sisters. Maybe we'll make up our own
secret family—with a dog!
XOXO

Then school started again. I checked under the stone on my way in. My note was still there. I put it in my pocket, figuring I'd give it to Tracy at school.

There was a snowball fight going on in the yard when I arrived. Mitchell got all ready to fire one at me, then lowered his hand.

"You better check on your friend," he said.

"What?"

"Tracy. She's around the corner, crying."

"You didn't do anything to her, did you?" I almost called him a creep, right there to his face, but I'm glad I didn't now.

He shook his head, and all of a sudden, he didn't seem like such a creep after all. He walked me to the corner of the building and pointed to where Tracy was leaning against the wall in her long brown coat, with her back to us.

"Tracy?" I called, making my way toward her over the snowdrifts that had blown up against that side of the building. "What's up?"

"Go away," she muttered.

"It's *me! Lindsay,*" I told her, still making my way closer.

"What's the matter?" I held out the note as I reached her, expecting her to read it and smile.

The next thing I knew, she'd spun around and slapped me across the face with her bare hand. "I said go away!" she cried. Before I could do or say anything, she took off across the yard and out the gate.

I sank to my knees in the snow, tears blurring her dark figure as it raced down the street. My cheek was throbbing where she'd hit me, but my feelings hurt a lot worse.

Mitchell saw it all happen and brought Mrs. Cooper around to where I was trying to dig a tissue out of my book bag with freezing hands. By then, I was crying pretty hard, I guess. And my nose was running. The note disappeared for good, trampled under the snow.

Behind Mitchell and Mrs. Cooper came half the school. I could hear the story growing: "That weird girl hit her, right in the eye." "She poked her eye out!" "She's going blind!"

"Everyone please take five giant steps back!" Mrs. Cooper ordered. "And stay there!" She waited to see that her directions were followed, then helped me to my feet.

I kept my head down, mainly to hide my runny nose. "I'm not blind," I muttered. "I just need a tissue, please."

Mrs. Cooper had one out of her pocket in no time and led me past the gawkers and inside the school. We went straight to the principal's office, where she found me a whole box of tissues. I gave my nose a good blow and then explained what had happened as best as I could. The secretary said Mr. Krantz, the principal, was at a school-board meeting, so Mrs. Cooper called Tracy's house.

"She's home," she told me as she hung up the phone. "Her mother says she's not feeling well. I'm afraid we'll have to leave it at that until she comes back to school."

"She did say she was sick over the holiday."

Mrs. Cooper cupped my chin in her hands and inspected my cheek. "I don't think not feeling well justifies slapping a friend," she said. "We'll get the nurse to give you an icepack."

Tracy didn't come back the next day or the day after that. Meanwhile, the slap changed everything. My mom, who is usually very sensible and understanding, got furious and said I was never to play with Tracy again. My classmates, including Mitchell and his sidekicks, turned all kind and sympathetic toward me, as if I were a war hero or something, and Tracy was the enemy.

Mrs. Cooper and I were the only ones on the exact same wavelength: We were worried about her. The slap wasn't anywhere near as big a deal as the *reason* she had slapped me, and we couldn't figure out that reason. Mrs. Cooper called Tracy at home every day—or had Mr. Krantz do it—and all they found out was that she still wasn't feeling well. As for me, I couldn't help checking behind our special stone every morning on my way to school and every afternoon on the way home. There was never anything there.

Then I got my third brilliant idea: Maybe Tracy was checking behind the stone, too, and not finding anything from me. So I left her a note. "I miss you," it said.

And I did. There'd been weeks of giggles, after all, and only one slap.

The next Friday, nearly two weeks after that day in the schoolyard, there was another scrap of notebook paper waiting for me behind the stone.

Hi—

I miss you, too.

    I'm sorry I hit you. I was just so angry—not at you, at the whole world.

    Everyone was talking about their happy holidays with their families, and mine was so bad. I can't tell anyone about this—only you. My family is not like yours or anybody else's. My stepdad hurts my mom. A lot. And sometimes he hurts me. That's why I can't come back to school right now.

    So no one will know.

    Please don't say anything.

    XOXO

Mom was still at work and Davey was at daycare when I got home. I crawled under the covers on my bed and read the note again, about a dozen times. Tracy's stepdad had no business hurting her or keeping her home to hide it! No wonder she never wanted to talk about anything outside of school!

At last I understood. And now, she'd asked me to help her keep this horrible secret.

When I heard Mom and Davey come into the house, I buried the note in a shoebox at the back of my closet. It stayed there all weekend. But hiding it didn't keep me from thinking and wondering and worrying about what it said.

Why didn't she want me to say anything? Was she afraid he'd hurt her more?

But if I didn't tell anyone, he'd still hurt her and who would stop him?

Daylight was just creeping in through my miniblinds on

Monday morning when another thought sat me bolt upright in bed, my heart pounding: *How could I lie to Mrs. Cooper?*

There'd be no getting around it. Mom would be easy; she never said another word about Tracy. But for days, Mrs. Cooper and I had asked one another about her every morning. Even after we gave up on that, as soon as I walked in the classroom, she'd tilt her head a little, and I could tell she was still wondering. So I'd shake my head "no." And so would she. And then she'd smile and look sad at the same time.

I couldn't ignore her, and I couldn't just go on shaking my head in the same way. But how could I admit I'd heard from Tracy and then pretend everything was fine?

I got dressed and dragged myself down to the kitchen. Mom was pouring Cheerios into a bowl for Davey.

"If someone tells you something," I said, "and she asks you not to tell anyone else, but you don't actually make that promise out loud, does that mean you're allowed to tell?"

Mom thought that over. "Possibly," she said, drawing the word out slowly.

I was hoping she'd say "Of course!"

I sat down and took my turn with the Cheerios. I couldn't look Mom in the eye, but I knew she was watching me.

I tried again: "Which is worse, lying or breaking a promise?"

I reached for the milk, but Mom stopped me, covering my hand with her own. "What's up, Lindsay?" she said.

I couldn't answer. If I opened my mouth, I'd blurt out everything, and I wasn't ready to do that yet.

"Some promises are a mistake," Mom went on. "And anyway, mothers are exempt."

"What's 'exempt'?" I asked, still not looking at her.

"When it comes to promises, mothers don't count. We're the exception to the rule. You're allowed to tell me what's wrong."

Tracy's note was tucked into the pocket of my jeans. I pulled it out and handed it over.

"Oh, my goodness," Mom cried. "I should have guessed! If only I hadn't been so angry about her hitting you!"

"You couldn't have guessed," I told her. "You never met Tracy. Mrs. Cooper didn't even guess."

"You need to show this note to Mrs. Cooper immediately," Mom said.

That's what I'd been longing to hear! I jumped up and gave her a long, hard hug. Tears of relief burned in my throat.

"Do you want me to come to school with you?" she asked. "I'll call the office and tell them I'll be late."

"No," I said. "I can handle it now."

Mom gave me another squeeze for good luck. "Mrs. Cooper will know what to do," she said.

Mrs. Cooper knew exactly what to do. She shared the note with Mr. Krantz, who called the Department of Family Services.

"They'll go to Tracy's house," she explained, back in our classroom. Everyone else had gone to Music. The empty room felt lonely. "If they confirm that Tracy's been mistreated, they'll have to remove her from the house."

"Where will she go?" I asked.

"To a foster home, most likely."

"But *where*?"

"Wherever there's room. It may be in the city. It may be out-side the county. Or out of state."

Tears were running down both of our faces now. I'd never seen a teacher cry. It was awful, but better than crying alone. Would Tracy have anyone to cry with her? She was so alone! And now she'd be in a strange place, far from her family, far from *me!*

"Maybe I shouldn't have told," I said.

Mrs. Cooper passed me a tissue and dabbed her own eyes with another. "If what Tracy says in that note is true," she said, "it's likely the situation would only get worse. *Dangerously* so. You did the right thing, Lindsay. You have to believe that."

Well, I would have to try. There was no taking it back now. "How long will she have to stay," I asked, "in that foster home?"

"That depends," Mrs. Cooper said. "If they can work with Tracy's mom to improve the situation, a judge will send her home. Otherwise, she'll stay in foster care—and maybe get adopted."

"But she already has a family!" I protested.

"Families are supposed to keep their children safe," Mrs. Cooper said.

And, of course, she was right.

Tracy never came back to our school, and I never heard from her again. I checked behind our stone every day until spring, when the empty lot was finally sold and the rubble cleared to make way for a new building.

We're moving again, when school's out for the summer, to a big old apartment building in Chicago. Mom and Davey and I went up for a long weekend to look it over. There are some old-fashioned houses in the neighborhood, and one of them has wind chimes hanging on the porch. I know I'll think of Tracy every time I hear them.

I'm still not one hundred percent sure I did the right thing. But I know I tried. I never got to be Tracy's pretend sister, but I did try to keep her safe.

Wherever she is, I hope she's getting a chance to giggle.

Emily Canarsie Has Something to Say

by Sue Corbett

The reason our neighborhood has a bookmobile is simple: Emily Canarsie made up her mind to win the summer reading contest, which had a grand prize of a karaoke party for ten friends. And once Emily makes up her mind, nothing will stop her, not even a naked man.

What happened was this: Emily and I were slurping soft-serve ice-cream cones on the Saturday before the last week of fifth grade, sitting on the only bench in the Tall Pines Shopping Center, right outside the library. She was talking, as usual. People thought Emily was quiet, but she had plenty to say when it was just us.

"You're dripping," I told her. I had been watching a chocolate peak collapse, wondering if she would ever notice it herself.

"Oops." Emily's tongue darted out, licking her fist first, then the cone. At that moment, she saw the poster, tacked up inside the library window.

"Rocket to Stardom with Reading," she said, getting up to examine the fine print. She dumped her cone in the trash and wiped her sticky hand on her backside. "I'm winning this! You coming, Maddie?" She didn't wait for an answer. By the time I had stuffed the rest of my cone in my mouth and crunched, Emily was inside.

Emily had always been what you'd call a Big Reader. That summer, she went kinda nuts. I think if Shari Andrews hadn't been in the contest, things might have been different, but Shari rubbed Emily the wrong way. The three of us were A students, but Shari wore her smarts like a tiara. She had won Citizen of the Year in fourth grade because she spent Saturday afternoons at a nursing home, reading newspaper stories to old folks. Emily couldn't hide her disgust the day the principal announced Shari's award.

"They make it out like she's a hero," Emily whispered, "when it's just another chance for Shari to listen to her favorite speaker."

Anyway, Emily got it in her fierce brain that she would win the contest—by a landslide. This meant a lot of trips to the library.

I like thick books because when I find a good one, I hate for it to end. But Emily went through books like other kids go through popcorn at the movies. She would find a writer she liked and *consume* everything that author ever wrote. In the *N*s, she found Phyllis Reynolds Naylor, the first author she had ever come across who had written enough to satisfy her appetite.

"I began to wonder if I would ever get to the *O*s," she said.

Mrs. Paciorek, the librarian, tacked up a chart on one wall. When we finished a book, we filled out an index card and Mrs. Paciorek would put a star above the rocket ships that bore our names. For the first month, Emily and Shari chased each other through the stratosphere, while I (and the rest of the summer readers) languished in the troposphere and below.

We were at the library twice a week, because there are only so many books you can carry when you're walking, and we were always walking. My parents worked and Emily's mother didn't "ferry" children around, as she put it, when God gave them legs for that purpose.

It was a *long* walk. Our town spreads out like a hand. Where we lived was on the knuckle of the thumb. The library was on the tip of the index finger. That might not sound far, but there's a wide highway between the thumb and the fingers. You can walk a mile out of the way to cross a bridge over the highway or you can cut through the woods.

We always cut through the woods. Our parents didn't know this, of course.

"Do NOT cut through the woods, Emily Louise," Mrs. Canarsie would warn, tucking a dollar for ice cream in the pocket of Emily's cutoffs. She would hold Emily by the pocket and shake her—for emphasis and to make the dollar go down—as she issued this warning. Emily was thin, rail thin, and you could see her hip bones wiggle inside her shorts when her mother did this.

"Y-y-yes, m-m-ma'am," Emily would say, in this fake vibrato.

The shortcut through the woods was cooler, too. A creek ran alongside the gravel path, and the canopy of elm and oak blocked out the sun. Reaching the neighborhood at the other end of the woods was like coming out of an air-conditioned store onto a desert.

The woods also gave us privacy. I shared a bedroom with Lucy, my older sister. The Canarsies had seven children, so Emily shared hers with *two* little sisters. Neither of us had any place to call our own. The summer before, we had rolled logs into a clearing off the path so we'd have a place to sit down.

"We can hang here without the cling-ons interrupting us," Emily said. Kerry and Clare were one part cute, two parts pest.

Another part of the woods' appeal was rooted in mystery. That spring we heard whispers about *something* in the woods— the details were left to our imaginations. I pressed my mother for specifics. She tut-tutted me.

"This can't possibly interest you, Maddie, because you are not *allowed* in the woods," she said. I reported this conversation to Emily.

"My brother says it's a troll who makes children work as slaves in his cave," Emily said, rolling her eyes. "Everyone knows there are no caves in those woods."

The woods were also quiet, which Emily liked. The Canarsies were a loud family. They lived across the street, and my parents often kept the living-room windows cranked shut because it's awkward to listen to people carry on like the Canarsies did.

In the woods, we heard just the noises we made and the *whoosh* of passing cars on the highway.

So when we were trudging home one day in late July, we both stopped at the distinct sound of a branch breaking.

"You hear that?" I asked. Emily nodded. We both looked around but saw only trees. We kept walking.

Then we heard a crunching noise, like shoes on dry leaves. We stopped and looked at each other without saying anything. My heartbeat picked up. I craned my neck left and right. "Probably an animal," I said. Emily was silent.

We didn't run. We were too cool for that. But we picked up our pace. I gripped my books tight to my chest.

I still don't know where he came from. In a flash he was in front of us, blocking our way on the path.

A man—scraggly-faced and balding.

His pants—underwear and all—dropped to his ankles.

I let out a strangled scream and froze. Emily gripped my arm to turn me around. "C'mon!" she yelled and took off running, pulling me behind her.

We charged through shortcuts, thorns and branches scratching our shins, racing back to the neighborhood by the library. Panting for air, we dropped to the curb when we reached the street.

"Is that . . . why we're not . . . supposed to be . . . in the woods?" I sputtered.

Emily's books had tumbled to the ground. She was bent in two, gasping. Finally, she straightened and blew out a big breath. "Don't tell your parents."

"Are you crazy? We *have* to tell our parents!"

"But then they'll know we've been in the woods!"

She had me there. "Did he follow us?"

Emily shook her head. My *body* shook—in fright.

When our breath came back, we walked home—the long way.

"Do you think he was going to hurt us?" I asked. Really, I was terrified.

"I think he's a wacko," Emily said.

The next week, we went the long way twice, arriving at the library feeling melted, like ice cream that's been left out too long.

Friday afternoon we both fell asleep on the couches in the children's room. I woke up to Mrs. Paciorek softly calling my name.

"We're closing in fifteen minutes, Maddie," she said.

Emily had reached the thermosphere while Shari Andrews appeared stuck in the mesosphere. (We later learned she had been on vacation.) I hoped Emily's lead meant fewer trips, but Monday morning I found her on my stoop again, books in hand. I had a plan, though.

"Lucy said she'll take us with her to the mall if we promise not to be her shadow." My sister had gotten her driver's license and was constantly running errands.

"But there are only two weeks left in the contest!"

"Em, it's too hot to walk all that way."

"We could cut through the woods," she suggested. I violently shook my head.

"Well, I am not going to let the Naked Man rule my life," she said, stomping off. She looked back at me, once, but I didn't relent. I did watch her, though. She headed to the woods.

The mall was a letdown. It's no fun to go by yourself. And I couldn't help worrying that Emily would run into the Naked Man again.

So you can imagine how fast my pulse got when my sister turned onto our street, and I saw a police car in the Canarsies' driveway.

"Wonder what that's about," Lucy said. I wondered if Emily was okay. Then I worried that, if she was, I was no longer her friend.

I was out of the car before Lucy shut off the engine. I raced across the street and into Emily's backyard through the opening in the hedges. I threw pebbles at her window until Clare appeared.

"Get Emily," I whispered, then put my finger to my lips so she'd know not to shout.

"She's in trouble," Clare whispered back.

"Can she come to the window?" Clare nodded and disappeared, just as Kerry's head popped up.

"She's in *big* trouble!" Kerry added. My stomach did a flipflop. At least she was alive.

A few moments later, there was Emily. "The police took my statement!"

"What happened?" I had climbed onto the picnic table to be closer to the second floor.

"When I got to the woods, guess who I found?" She turned her head to glare at Kerry, who shrank away. "The pests!" she spat. "Sitting on *our* logs! So I had to bring them home, and then I had to tell my mother, because I was afraid they'd go there again. She called the police."

"Are you grounded for life?"

"Till school starts. But my father is madder at the police than me because the Naked Man has been in the woods for months!"

"Well, I'll be grounded, too, as soon as my parents find out."

"No, I told my mother I was by myself, looking for a place to read."

I couldn't believe how lucky I was to have a friend who knew when to shut up.

Emily was not allowed out even to go to the library, so I walked the long way around twice that week to get books, which we hoisted up to her room in a backpack tied to a rope she lowered out of the window.

"Where's Shari?" she asked.

"Thermosphere, but you're still ahead."

She gave me the thumbs-up sign.

A few nights later the doorbell rang.

"Can you come to the City Council meeting?" Emily asked breathlessly. "My father's going to make a stink about the Naked Man."

I looked around the house nervously. Since Emily hadn't mentioned I had seen the Naked Man, too, the Canarsies hadn't said anything to my parents. I was hoping the whole thing would just go away. "Hang on," I said and went to tell my mother I was going out with Emily and her dad.

We sat in the back of the meeting room. The mayor and city council sat on a dais up front. The police chief, fire chief, and some other people sat at long tables. We recited the Pledge. Then we listened to a solid hour of debates about garbage rates and property taxes.

Finally, the mayor called Mr. Canarsie's name. "Please come up to the microphone," the mayor advised. The other council people smiled.

Mr. Canarsie started calmly, telling Emily's version of events. By the end, he was jabbing his finger into the air and shouting. "How come my *daughter* can find this weirdo and the police can't? This guy's been flashing people since LAST summer."

Emily and I looked at each other, wide-eyed. Everybody on the dais straightened their shoulders and grimaced. "Sir, please," the mayor said, rapping his gavel. "Let's be civil. Our police tried to catch the flasher, but he hasn't been sighted in months and, frankly, it's up to parents to supervise their children. . . ."

"How dare you blame this on parents!" a councilwoman cut in. "You were the one who didn't want to tell the news media about the flasher last fall!"

The mayor's face reddened. A third councilman started quizzing the police chief, who said he was understaffed because of the requirement for "two-man patrols." That started a squabble about the police union's contract!

"I think they've forgotten what the subject is," I whispered to Emily.

"Would you have gone through the woods if you had known about the Naked Man?" she asked me. I shook my head.

"In a way, it's a good thing we didn't know."

"You wouldn't be in the exosphere right now, that's for sure."

"C'mon." She got up and tugged my arm to make me stand up.

"Where are we going, Em?" I asked in alarm. She ignored me, heading up the aisle to the microphone, pulling me behind her.

"Excuse me," she said to the police chief. He seemed thrilled to step aside. Emily cleared her throat into the microphone.

"Young lady?" the mayor asked.

"My name is Emily Canarsie," she said, pausing for effect. "And I have something to say."

You could have heard a branch break as Emily spoke. She started with the summer reading contest. She explained about the long walk. She told the council about her run-in with the Naked Man. I sneaked a peek at her father, who was standing off to the side. He looked startled. I bet he had never heard Emily say so much before.

"So the woods are off-limits. We *all* know that now," Emily told them. "But the library is still on one side of town and I live on the other. The Naked Man is keeping me from the books." She put her hands on her hips. "Fortunately, I have an idea."

The bookmobile arrived the next week. Emily and I were at the corner of Violet and Roosevelt when it pulled up.

"You must be Emily," the driver said, opening the door. "And you're the famous sidekick, right? Maddie?"

We nodded and climbed aboard. It was cool inside, and the driver let us sit on the bench seat in the front and read the entire time she was parked there. She also brought us index cards and took the completed ones back to Mrs. Paciorek. Emily won the summer reading contest, hands down. She even invited Shari Andrews to the karaoke party. Shari sang a solo. Emily rolled her eyes. Then she and I did a duet.

See, after Emily's speech, a newspaper reporter cornered her for an interview. Standing there listening, I realized even though Emily was saying as little as possible, she was going to be a celebrity by morning.

More important, I realized I had some talking to do myself.

"I'm gonna tell my mom and dad," I said to Emily when we got home.

She nodded. "We should've told them the day it happened. You were right about that, Maddie." We hugged and I knew, no matter how much trouble I was going to be in at home, Emily and I were fine.

I got grounded for the rest of the summer, too, but my parents said they were glad I had told the truth and relieved nothing bad had happened to us.

Emily's picture was in the paper, with a report on the city council voting to add bookmobile service to our neighborhood immediately. (The paper also had a little pencil sketch of the Naked Man and, a few weeks later, the police picked him up.)

Mid-morning, I took the newspaper to the living room, intending to clip the article for my scrapbook. Out the front window, I saw Channel Four's satellite truck roll up to the Canarsies'. Within minutes, every kid on the block spilled onto the sidewalk. A cameraman got out with a blonde lady I recognized as one of the reporters on Channel Four. The two of them marched up the Canarsies' walk. Mrs. Canarsie came out, then some of the Canarsie kids and, finally, Emily.

I was *dying* to go over there myself when next thing I knew, this whole parade of people, led by Emily, was crossing the street. I opened the door before Emily could ring the bell.

"Channel Four wants to know about the city council meeting." She leaned closer. *"It's your turn,"* she said in an insistent whisper.

I looked at the TV lady. She smiled and nodded to her cameraman, who hit a button. A red light came on and the TV lady tilted her microphone toward me.

"Go ahead, Maddie," Emily said. "Tell the story."

So I did.

The Wind Will Know Your Name

by Patricia Calvert

As she ran down the narrow path into Crazy Horse Coulee, Katie saw Grandmother hanging the wash over two strands of barbed wire, the remnants of a pasture that once held a few horses and a couple of cows. The wind—it always blew in the coulee—flattened the old woman's faded blue dress against her stick-thin body and teased strands of hair from the silver braid hanging down her back.

"I'm home, Grandmother!" Katie called. Grandmother didn't turn to greet her. Katie hadn't expected she would.

The old woman's hearing was so poor that most of the time she was a prisoner in a silent world. She never heard the songs carried by the wind or a redtail's sharp cry as it circled overhead. If you looked straight at Grandmother when you spoke, though, you could make yourself understood. Only when Digger dashed past the old woman and charged up the slope, his red tail raised like a ragged banner over his skinny back, did Grandmother turn to see who was coming.

Katie waved. Grandmother raised one arm straight into the air in reply, five fingers spread wide against the hard blue prairie sky. The question rose up in front of Katie, as it often did lately, "What will happen to me when something happens to her?" Deep in her bones she knew it wasn't a matter of *if* something happened to Grandmother. It was only a matter of when.

Katie darted around the answer as if it were a *sinte,* a snake, coiled and ready to strike. The social-worker people from the Bureau of Indian Affairs would descend on Crazy Horse Coulee like grasshoppers, that's what would happen.

They would take one look at the barbed-wire fence with its scraps of faded wash, at the rusty tin roof on the shack huddled near the creek, at the skeletons of dead cars along the rim of the coulee, then they'd take her away. "For your own good," they would say. As if people who worked in offices with records in their computers knew what was best for everyone else. Long ago, the Lakotas didn't have to ask permission from anyone— not government officials or the chief of any other tribe—to go wherever or do whatever they wished. That was a time only someone as old as Grandmother could remember.

"Taya, taya!" Katie cried. "Hello, hello!" She ran to hug Grandmother. The old woman's shoulders poked up as sharp as antelope antlers under her cotton dress. Beneath Katie's fingers, the knobs of her grandmother's spine felt as smooth as river pebbles. Age had creased the old woman's brown cheeks so deeply they looked more like the hide of a lizard than human skin.

Grandmother smiled, showing a round, dark hole in her face. She'd lost her teeth long before Mama died, before Katie came to live at Crazy Horse Coulee. The dentures the government clinic gave her fit poorly, so she wore them only a few times. She put them on a shelf next to the stove, where they grinned cheer-fully at friends and strangers alike.

"Oh, Grandmother, I wish there was a way to buy some col-ored pencils and drawing paper!" Katie exclaimed, holding the old woman at arm's length and speaking directly to her. "Then I could practice drawing even when I'm not in school." She'd meant to bring up the subject later, when Grandmother was making fry bread for supper, but the wind peeled the words off her lips and tossed them into the air before she could snatch them back.

"Pencils? Paper?" Grandmother echoed, her voice as faded as her dress.

"Mr. Finch says I have talent, Grandmother. There's going to be an art fair in Bismarck, and he told me I should—"

"Talent?" Grandmother repeated the word slowly. "We hardly have money for food," she reminded Katie.

It was true. Katie knew it as well as Grandmother. She turned away, sorry she'd brought it up, and headed for the shack. As she stepped through the door, she felt Grandmother's cool, thin hand rest lightly on her arm.

"I have saved something," she announced in a voice sud-denly not thin or faded at all. "Maybe you could sell it. It might bring you enough for those things you want, those pencils and that paper."

Katie looked around the single room she'd shared with Grandmother for the past four years, ever since Mama died in the government hospital. Tuberculosis, the doctor had called it. Katie knew perfectly well Mama died because she didn't want to live anymore. (The government people didn't have an official word for broken hearts.) With Papa dead long before, then

Mama gone, it meant she was an orphan, a *wablenica*. Grandmother had been the only one to turn to. The shack in Crazy Horse Coulee was the only place left to call home.

Katie knew every square inch of the room. She felt her mouth go dry. There wasn't anything here anyone would buy.

Grandmother's bed, its crooked metal headboard scaly with peeling white paint, stood in one corner. Her own cot—a lumpy mattress laid on top of an old door that had been rescued from a shed out back and propped up on wood blocks—stood in the opposite corner. A wire suspended between the beds held some of the clothes she and Grandmother owned—another thin dress and a jacket for Grandmother, an extra pair of jeans and two shirts for herself.

The kitchen table, one of its four legs a quarter-inch shorter than the others, making it wobble like Grandmother herself, sat in the middle of the room. A fire hadn't been built yet in the black iron stove against the west wall, because the May sun on the tin roof had made the shack almost too warm for comfort. When summer came, the heat would be unbearable; then she and Grandmother would sleep outside under the star-pocked dome of the black prairie sky.

Nothing here to sell. Nothing.

Katie's shoulders collapsed like folded wings around her heart. It had been delicious to imagine winning a blue ribbon, its edges crisp and pleated, at the art fair Mr. Finch had talked about. Yet even as she'd dreamed the dream, Katie knew it was only that—a dream that couldn't come true.

"I have kept this a long time," Grandmother murmured, tottering on swollen feet to the side of her bed. She lifted up the worn *sina,* the quilt, and reached into a hole in the side of the mattress. She took out something flat, wrapped in brown paper, and held it against her chest.

"I meant to give this to you someday, Katie. Now is the right time." Grandmother's narrow black eyes were hard as flint in their nets of wrinkles.

"The *wasichus,* the whites, wish to buy such things. They crave to own pieces of our history, then tell themselves they know all about us." Her words were as sharp as a rabbit stick as she held the parcel out to Katie. "Someone will give you good money for this, enough to buy the things you need."

Katie loosened the brown paper. The frame around the photograph was made of deerskin and emboidered with porcupine quills dyed yellow, black, red, and white, the sacred colors of the Lakota. Katie stared at the girl in the picture. She was a stranger. Younger than Katie was herself, maybe only eight or nine years old. She wore a doeskin dress, fringed at the hem. A bone necklace hung around her neck, and she held a turkey-feather fan at her side. She returned Katie's stare across time and space with a steady gaze.

"This is *my* grandmother," Grandmother said. "That means she's your great-great-grandmother. Long ago, when we of the *Otchenti Chakowin,* the Seven Council Fires, came to live on places called reservations, a white man came with a camera. He took many pictures, and my grandmother's was one of them." Grandmother touched the face of the girl in the picture with a finger twisted by arthritis.

"When you were born, I asked your mother to give you my grandmother's name. I didn't want it to be lost, as so many things have been lost to us. If the name became yours, I knew the wind would remember it."

"She was called Katie, too?" Katie whispered, unable to take her eyes from those of the girl in the picture.

"Not in the beginning. Back then, she was called Blue Thunder, a name filled with good medicine," Grandmother said. "The old ones believed if thunder was heard when the sky was blue it meant the spirits were keeping watch." The old woman inspected the picture more closely.

"It was when the whites sent my grandmother to the mission school that they added the name Katie. After that, she was always called Katie Blue Thunder."

Katie Blue Thunder.

Moments ago, Katie's heart had felt so *asilya*, so sad. Now it filled up with something sweet and rare. Grandmother had held the picture against her heart; Katie did the same before she gave it back.

"Put this away, Grandmother. We will never sell it," she vowed. "Not to anyone. Not for food, not for pencils or paper either. If we get hungry, I'll help you gather prairie turnips. We'll make soup out of sage leaves and wild onions. I'll hunt for birds' eggs. I'll learn to throw a rabbit stick, like Grandfather did—but we won't sell our past."

Without wrapping the photograph in the brown paper, Grandmother slipped it back into its hiding place. Then she smoothed the wrapping paper out on top of the wobbly table. "It isn't the kind you wanted, but can you use this to practice on?"

"Yes," Katie said, partly to make Grandmother happy, mostly because it was better than no paper at all. There even was enough to make more than one picture. Before she began to draw, Katie went out to the yard and found a small, flat stone to put under the table leg to keep it from wobbling. It didn't matter if the table jiggled when they ate supper, but it needed to be steady if a person wanted to make pictures. She fished a three-inch stub of drawing pencil out of the pocket of her jeans and sat down.

"What will you make a picture of?" Grandmother asked as she sifted flour to make fry bread.

Katie studied the room, the two beds, the table, the stove. Digger lay in the doorway, asleep, his tail a limp red flag. Beyond the open door—there was no screen, so flies and Digger came and went as they pleased—she saw the rim of Crazy Horse Coulee, the carcasses of old cars, the sandhills in the distance. She watched as Grandmother stuffed willow twigs in the stove and started a cook fire.

"Of you," Katie said. She began to draw. The pencil stub flew across the paper with a mind of its own. Grandmother came to life: Her dress fell in folds around her body, her single braid trailed down her back, her swollen feet overran her slippers.

Grandmother came to lean over Katie's shoulder. "Is that what I look like?" she asked, surprised.

"It is how I see you, Grandmother," Katie said.

"That woman is *old*!" Grandmother exclaimed, indignant.

"You are old, Grandmother."

"I know, I know." Grandmother sighed, her voice drifting away. "Once, when my hair was as black as yours, Blue Thunder told me stories about the time of no fences, no roads, no place called a reservation. The people of the Seven Council Fires went freely everywhere, as did the deer and the antelope. Blue Thunder told me—" Grandmother paused and was silent.

"What did she tell you, Grandmother?" The best thing about living in Crazy Horse Coulee was listening to Grandmother's tales about how things used to be. Grandmother poured cooking oil in a fry pan and began to roll out the bread. As she worked, she began a story about the day Blue Thunder put on a doeskin dress the color of milk, mounted a fine painted pony, and rode to meet Eagle Catcher, her beloved. Katie listened, let the words and names wash over her, and savored the rich smell of frying bread.

After art class, Mr. Finch studied the picture of Grandmother for so long that Katie's palms got slick with sweat. If only she'd had better paper, not old, crackly brown wrapping paper. She should have drawn a picture of Digger, or even of the bare sandhills, not of a lean old woman with a braid hanging down her back. Mr. Finch must think the picture of Grandmother—the thin dress hiding none of her scrawniness, her cheeks hollow because her teeth smiled down from a shelf—was so ugly he couldn't think of anything to say.

"It's a fine piece of work, Katie," he said at last.

"It was the only paper I had," she explained.

"That's part of the charm of this portrait," Mr. Finch said with a smile. He called it a *portrait,* not a mere picture. "Who is this lady?"

"My grandmother," Katie said.

"The paper you used is as thoroughly itself as your grandmother is. Some artists would say it was a lucky accident it's all you had."

Strange! To think an accident could be lucky. The ones Katie knew about—Papa drinking too much at the Crossroads Bar six years ago on a bitter January night, falling into a ditch beside the road, then freezing to death before morning—weren't the lucky kind.

"I have an old box of colored pencils in my desk," Mr. Finch said. "I haven't used them in a long while. Would you like to take them home and experiment with them? I have some paper you can have, too."

Katie's face felt hot. She bent her head so Mr. Finch couldn't see the bright spots she knew had bloomed on her cheeks. "That would be *ayuco*," she whispered. "That would be very good."

Mr. Finch collected the pencils from his desk. Several were like the piece she already had, hardly more than stubs, but the colors were still bright. "Here's a sharpener, too," he said, adding a blue plastic one like little kids used in first grade. He found several sheets of paper in another drawer, a few tinted pale blue, peach, yellow, or gray. "Sometimes a colored ground—you know, a tinted background—can add a special effect to an artist's work," he said.

An artist's work. Mr. Finch said it as if he considered she was one already. Only three words, but Katie tucked them away to be taken out later. She'd polish them, as she'd polished the agate she found in the creek last summer. She'd rubbed it until it gleamed and kept it in a tin can next to her bed. She'd do the same with Mr. Finch's words, polish them until they gleamed.

When Katie leaped down the slope into Crazy Horse Coulee after school, Digger ran to meet her, more eager than usual. The sky was still blue, but overnight the prairie weather had turned sharply cold. Katie was surprised to see that no smoke curled up from the crooked chimney poking out of the tin roof of the shack beside the creek.

She ran in, breathless, to find Grandmother standing at the fly-specked window next to the unlit stove.

"I've been waiting for you," she said. She smiled, the round cavity in her wrinkled face as dark as the entrance of a cave.

"Look, Grandmother!" Katie exclaimed. "See what Mr. Finch gave me—pencils in every color—paper, and a sharpener, too!"

Grandmother shuffled to the table and studied the things Katie had spread out. "Now you have what you need, Katie," she said. "It's because I heard thunder behind the sandhills today. I knew the spirits were looking out for you."

When Katie turned, she saw Grandmother lightly tap her own chest with a gnarled middle finger. She looked past Katie's shoulder, out the door, which was open, as if she saw something coming. Katie turned. Maybe three or four *sungnini,* wild horses, had come to the creek for water. If they had, she'd catch them on paper, their manes and tails thick as ropes, their eyes wild and white-ringed.

She felt Grandmother lean against her and reached out to steady the old woman. Grandmother's breath brushed her cheek as lightly as a butterfly's wing.

"Are you dizzy, Grandmother?" Katie asked. "Let me help you lie down. It always makes you feel better, remember?" She guided her grandmother toward the bed with its peeling metal frame and lifted the old woman's legs onto the quilt. Grandmother's ankles were darker and puffier than usual, and her flesh was cool.

"You'll be all right in a moment, Grandmother," Katie promised. She knew she was speaking more to herself than to Grandmother. "You should have waited for me to haul water from the creek," she scolded gently, "but I will make our supper tonight so that you can rest."

Grandmother sighed, folded her hands across her narrow

chest, and closed her eyes. Katie watched as the lines in the old woman's face eased, almost the same way the wrinkles had been smoothed out of the brown wrapping paper yesterday.

"Don't be afraid, Katie Blue Thunder," Grandmother whispered. "No matter where you go, or what kind of pictures you draw, the wind will always know your name."

What will happen to me when something happens to her?

It was the question Katie had darted around for four years, as if it were a rattlesnake coiled under a clump of sagebrush. She knelt beside the bed, rested her hand on Grandmother's arm, and saw the blue fabric of the old woman's dress rise and fall with her shallow breaths. Digger came close, and Katie felt him press his shoulder against her hip. She laid her right hand against the smooth crown of Digger's head.

The light in the room dimmed. A fire should be started soon. She'd make fry bread for supper. She'd remember to haul extra water from the creek so Grandmother wouldn't need to do anything tomorrow.

Katie wasn't sure when the blue fabric covering Grandmother's chest ceased to move, when the shallow breathing stopped. When she realized it had, she stayed right where she was, on her knees beside the bed, one hand on Grandmother's arm, the other resting on Digger's head.

"Don't be afraid," Grandmother had said. Katie swallowed hard. A fly buzzed against the window next to the stove. Cold air slithered across the floor like a *sinte*. Digger whined softly.

"I won't, Grandmother," Katie whispered. But she was.

The social-worker people were almost kind when they came. The tallest one was even Lakota. No one announced—not right away, anyway—that they knew what was best for her. "Don't worry. We'll find a place for you" was all they said.

"What about Digger?" Katie asked. He was Grandmother's dog. Without her, he was a *wablenica,* too.

"You won't be able to take the dog with you," one of the social workers answered briskly.

"Of course she can," said the tall one who was Lakota.

When Mr. Finch brought the blue ribbon back from the art fair in Bismarck, it looked just like the one Katie had imagined in her dreams—shiny, its edges crisp and pleated. "This is only the first of many prizes you'll win," he said. Katie felt her cheeks get warm; this time she didn't lower her head.

The picture she'd drawn of Grandmother on a piece of light blue paper was the way she wanted to remember her. Not lying motionless on a bed whose metal headboard was scaly with peeling paint, but a lean woman who stood tall, her hand raised high in the air, five fingers spread against the hard prairie sky, a thin dress pressed flat against her body.

Beyond Grandmother were the skeletons of cars on the rim of Crazy Horse Coulee. Farther away, in the sandhills, were swiftly sketched figures to show that *sungnini* were still out there, running wild and free.

In the right-hand corner of the drawing, Katie had added her name. Katie Blue Thunder. The wind would remember her, even after she'd followed one of the roads that led away from the reservation like the spokes from a wheel.

Un/titled

by Edwidge Danticat

I come to this party
Un/invited
I am not of the tribe of the ink
My people were not scribes
My grandfather's entire tale
Was scribbled in hieroglyphics
On his birth papers
His father's and his name misspelled
(From this all of his children
Ended up with his middle name
As surnames)
So please forgive me
But this is why I am at this party
Bearing the wrong name.

I come to this party
With no poetic legacy
(But plenty of license)
No plot of land on any mound
To cradle my willfulness
My entire tale
Hovering now

Over the white spaces
On this page.

I come to this party
To buy a vowel
To help decipher my memory
To borrow a theory
From one of the sages
To explain
Why I won't cower
Why I won't shut up
Why I will never ask permission
Not to shut up.

I come to this party
To answer "PRESENT"
At the roll call of my own oblivion
For I am coming to this party
Through a careless crack
At the back door
An accident of literacy
Still clinging to a pencil
That I wouldn't let go
Even when
There was no one around
From whom to borrow
A single line.

The Contributors and Their Work

The photographs in this section show the authors at ages nine to thirteen.

ELAINE MARIE ALPHIN created stories as a child even before she could write them down. Now her novel *Ghost Cadet* has won Virginia's Best Book Award, *Ghost Soldier* was nominated for the Edgar Award for Best Juvenile Mystery (and won  the Society of Midland Authors Award for Children's Fiction), and *Counterfeit Son* won the Edgar. Younger readers will also enjoy *A Bear for Miguel,* set in El Salvador.

About "New World Dreams"
"My father came to America from El Salvador as a teenager, and my mother's family came to America from Ireland. As a history student, I found myself wondering about all the different types of people who came to the New World with dreams. It seemed to me that those who came with the greatest dreams, and the most at risk, were those who chose to bind their futures to the New World by coming here as indentured servants. So I combined their history with my family dreams and came up with Katie's story."

SANDY ASHER began making up plays and acting them out with friends in second grade. *A Woman Called Truth,* her best-known published play, has been produced at more than 250 theaters around the country, in Canada, and in Australia and won the Distinguished Play Award from the American Alliance for Theatre and Education. She has also published two dozen books for young readers, including *Stella's Dancing Days*.

About "The Secret Behind the Stone"
"When I was in elementary school, one of my classmates suddenly slapped me across the face—for no apparent reason. I remember my teacher holding me while I cried, and I remember the other girl lifting her blouse to reveal red welts crisscrossing her back. I had no idea what those welts meant. Even if I'd understood that she'd been hurt, I wouldn't have known what to do about it. People didn't talk about such things at that time. But now I understand. That's why I wrote this story."

DR. MIRIAM BAT-AMI is a professor of children's literature at Western Michigan University. Her novel *Dear Elijah* says a lot about the way she was when she started counting her age in double digits. She wanted a way to talk to God using a language that made sense to her. Another of her novels, *Two Suns in the Sky*, is a World War II romance. It won the Scott O'Dell Award.

About "This Is the Way It Is"
"I have a horse, and I ride her a couple of times a week. Sometimes, when we're riding right, I do feel special, like the narrator in this poem. I also love the way you can be at a barn. Horse women are strong, and they love it that way. I am also a proud brainiac."

MARION DANE BAUER is the author of more than thirty books for young people and has won numerous awards, including a Newbery Honor Award for her novel *On My Honor*. Her ALA Notable Book,

What's Your Story? A Young Person's Guide to Writing Fiction, is used by writers of all ages. Her most recent novels are *Runt,* the story of a wolf pup; *Land of the Buffalo Bones,* part of Scholastic's Dear America series; and *The Double-Digit Club.* Ms. Bauer is on  the faculty of the Master of Fine Arts in Writing for Children and Young Adults program of Vermont College.

About "Rabbit Stew"

"I encountered this story in an anecdote about a real-life trick played on one boy by some other boys. I thought the incident marvelously funny, especially the laughing Indian in it when the whites who traveled through their lands were so convinced that Indians never laughed. In the real incident, the Indian did not provide the rabbits, nor was it a girl on whom the joke was played. But since girls were still hobbled by restrictive ideas of what women could and could not do, despite the fact that they had to face every hardship the men did on that arduous journey, I enjoyed making the encounter an affirming one for a young girl."

BONNY BECKER has published a number of books, including a funny picture book called *The Christmas Crocodile* and the novel *My Brother the Robot.* Ms. Becker grew up in a small town in east-  ern Washington and now lives in Seattle with her husband and two teenaged daughters. She's been a writer for as long as she can remember and loves stories with a little bit of magic and oddness to them.

About "The Makeover"

"We live near a middle school and a high school. Watching my kids and the kids in the schools, it struck me how terribly important popularity is at a certain age. It also struck me that being popular is hard.

You're almost obligated to gossip and party and maintain this social frenzy around yourself. Gossip and meanness can be fun in a weird, awful way—but at some level, I think people who do this hate that about themselves—only they can't get off the merry-go-round. All these thoughts spun around in my head to turn into 'The Makeover.'"

PATRICIA CALVERT wanted to be a writer even though she had great difficulty learning to read because of dyslexia. Ms. Calvert's main characters also face rocky roads in their lives, but her books have won many honors: the Christopher Award *(Glennis,*
Before and After), Bank Street Book of the Year *(Bigger),* Junior Literary Guild *(Picking Up the Pieces),* and ALA Best Book *(Yesterday's Daughter).*

About "The Wind Will Know Your Name"
"I grew up in Montana, a state with many reservations and a large Native American population, mostly Blackfeet. Near the city where I grew up—Great Falls—there was a small "undeclared" reservation, a sort of ghetto, in which local Indian families lived in shacks without electricity, plumbing, or running water. My family—as haunted by poverty as the ones in the ghetto—lived nearby. I knew several Native American kids in school. One of them was a girl named Anna. She was a tall, strong girl with terrific energy and deep belief in herself, who regularly won first place in all the girls' track events. After Anna dropped out of school, I never found out what happened to her—yet I think about her to this day."

SUE CORBETT has always been a Big Reader, which is why she loves her job as the children's book reviewer for the *Miami Herald*. She is a journalist and the author of the novel *12 Again*. She lives in Newport News, Virginia, with four other Big Readers—
her husband, Tom Davidson, and her children, Conor, Liam, and Brigit.

About "Emily Canarsie Has Something to Say"
"One of the things that motivated me to read was the public library's summer reading contest, which my sister and I took very seriously. My sister *consumed* books the way Emily does. She routinely ran away with the top reading prize. I wrote this story to honor that memory and explore the passion of a reader who will not let *anything* get between her and her books. My sister is also very good at knowing when to talk and when to shut up—a very valuable skill."

EDWIDGE DANTICAT was born in Port-au-Prince, Haiti, an island in the Caribbean. She is the author of three novels; one of them, *Behind the Mountains,* was written for young adults. She is also the author of a short-story collection, *Krik? Krak!,*  and a travel book called *After the Dance: A Walk Through Carnival in Jacmel, Haiti.*

About "Un/titled"
"A friend of mine once told me that he heard a rumor in my community that I wasn't the one who had written my books, that an old boyfriend of mine, a Ph.D. in Arts and Letters, had written them for me. This wasn't the first time I heard this. I realized that this rumor was circulating because I come from a poor rural family, and in many people's minds, people like me are not supposed to write books. I wrote this poem as a response."

VALISKA GREGORY is Writer-in-Residence at Butler University. Her books have received *Parents' Choice* Awards, been chosen as American Bookseller "Pick of the Lists," featured on PBS and national television, and translated into seven lan-  guages. She has two grown daughters and lives with her husband in Indianapolis.

About "Princess Isobel and the Pea"

"On Christmas Eve when I was ten, my Aunt Ann gave me the first two books I'd ever owned: *The Wonderful Wizard of Oz* and a collection of Grimm's fairy tales. I read the stories in those two treasured books over and over, and I've long wanted to retell some of the fairy tales as I wished they'd been written."

MARGARET PETERSON HADDIX is the author of many books, including *Running Out of Time, Just Ella, The Girl with 500 Middle Names, Because of Anya,* and the *Among the Hidden* series. Her books have been honored with an IRA Children's Book  Award; ALA Best Book for Young Adults notations; and more than a dozen state readers' choice awards. She lives with her husband and kids in Columbus, Ohio.

About "Bird"

"Once when I was eleven or twelve, I saw kids throwing stones at a baby bird that had fallen out of its nest. They were younger than I was; they probably would have stopped if I'd told them to. Yet I didn't have the courage to speak up.

"Years later, I was looking through a diary I'd kept when I was in sixth grade, and three words leaped out at me: 'The bird incident.' That was all I'd written—partly because I was too ashamed to spell it all out, and partly because my sixth-grade self had had full confidence that I would always remember what 'the bird incident' was. And I did. I remembered how guilty I'd felt, as if I'd thrown the stones myself. And I remembered how confused I'd been about why I didn't come to the bird's defense.

"So, in my story, I made Jeanie braver than I'd been. I even gave her greater odds than I'd faced: Though I did grow up on a farm, my father was never in danger of losing his land. I still wish I'd stood up to the stone-throwers. But maybe realizing my failures made me braver some other time. I hope it did."

PAMELA SMITH HILL grew up in Springfield, Missouri. She started writing stories in third grade and sold her first newspaper story when she was eighteen. Her lifelong dream of writing books came true with *Ghost Horses* in 1996. Other books  include *A Voice from the Border* and *The Last Grail Keeper.* Ms. Hill lives in Portland, Oregon. She teaches writing at Washington State University in Vancouver.

About "Where the Lilacs Grow"
"For years, I was haunted by one particular Sunday afternoon in the late 1960s, a day when I visited a friend's farm in Missouri that would soon be flooded by Stockton Lake, which was being created by the U.S. Army Corps of Engineers. My friend's family had moved their farmhouse to a sliver of land that the lake wouldn't flood. The house felt out of place in its new location, lonely and unsheltered. Then my friend and I walked up to the foundation where her house had once been, and two huge lilac bushes stood out front. How green and tall they were, how lovely. And yet, they'd never bloom again. By the following spring, they'd be underwater. My friend started to cry—and so did I.

"Now fishermen, campers, and hikers flock to Stockton Lake. Most of them probably don't know about the tremendous sacrifices families made so the government could build the dam that forms the lake. It's largely a forgotten story. So I wanted to return to that day long ago and bring that time and place back to life—for myself, but mostly for all the people whose homes and even towns are now underwater."

SARA HOLBROOK is the author of many books of poetry for young people, including *I Never Said I Wasn't Difficult, Walking on the Bound-*

aries of Change, and *Wham! It's a Poetry Jam.* She
began writing poetry for her two daughters when
they were young, sharing the poems with them as
a way of saying, "I understand." She is a perfor-
mance poet and has appeared before audiences
across the U.S. and abroad.

About "Girlfriends"
"I was actually thinking of how I communicate with my two daughters—how we can make ourselves understood to each other in a
crowded, noisy room or in a silent church, through the eloquence of
touch. And then I realized I can talk to my girlfriends the same way."

MARTHE JOCELYN grew up with a sister and two
brothers in Toronto, Canada. They liked to dress
up and perform shows in the backyard or the attic.
Ms. Jocelyn moved to New York City when she was
twenty and eventually started her own company,
designing toys and children's clothing. Reading to her two daughters
inspired her to write stories of her own. Her books include *Earthly
Astonishments* and *Mable Riley.*

About "The Palazzo Funeral Parlor"
"My daughters go to school across the street from a tiny storefront funeral parlor in Greenwich Village. While I waited to pick up my kids
one day, I noticed a woman leaning out of the window, watching a coffin being loaded into the hearse. That started me wondering what it
might be like to live in her apartment. . . ."

ANGELA JOHNSON won Coretta Scott King Awards for her books
Toning the Sweep and *Heaven.* When I Am Old with You and *The Other
Side* received Coretta Scott King Honor Awards. Other titles for young

readers include *A Cool Moonlight, Maniac Monkeys on Magnolia Street,* and *Running Back to Ludie,* a book of poetry. Ms. Johnson has received the Ezra Jack Keats New Writer Award, the PEN Norma Klein New Writer Award, and a MacArthur Foundation Fellowship.

About "A Girl Like Me"

"I believe I felt my most powerful at the age of eleven. I actually gleaned a bit of this poem from something I wrote in the sixth grade. Sixth grade for me was such a pivotal year. I made decisions that would see me through a lot of difficult social development. I held fast to those beliefs. I am what I thought I would be: someone who is strong and sure of my footing. I wrote 'A Girl Like Me' because I have a twelve-year-old niece who is in the midst of the struggle of adolescence. But she is strong, brilliant, and always searching, which is the best part."

SHEILA SOLOMON KLASS has written many books for young readers, including biographical novels about the unusual, challenging, and sometimes hilarious childhoods of two talented American women: Louisa May Alcott *(Little Women Next*

Door) and Annie Oakley *(A Shooting Star).* Ms. Klass teaches at Manhattan Community College and lives in New York City. All three of her children are writers.

About "Annie's Opinion"

"I wrote 'Annie's Opinion' because I was so impressed by Annie Oakley's triumph over a complicated and difficult childhood that, years after I finished the novel about her, I once again wanted to celebrate her strength and courage."

ROBIN MICHAL KOONTZ spent much of her early childhood in Tuscaloosa, Alabama. She is the illustrator-author of *Why a Dog? By a Cat* as well as many other picture books and early readers. "The Story Quilt" is her first story for middle-  graders. The 125-year-old quilt, made by her great-grandmother, is draped over Grandma Jennie's rocking chair in Ms. Koontz's house near Noti, Oregon.

About "The Story Quilt"
"I was inspired by loss. And I was inspired by the quilt of ten thousand pieces made by my great-grandmother. But most of all, I was inspired by all of the storytellers in my life, past and present."

FRANCESS LANTZ was born in Bucks County, Pennsylvania, and grew up wanting to be a writer. Her first novel was published in 1982, and she's been writing for children ever since. Her latest books include *Luna Bay: A Roxy Girl Series; Letters to*  *Cupid;* and *Stepsister from Planet Weird,* which was made into a Disney Channel Original Movie. Ms. Lantz lives in Santa Barbara, California, with her son and their dog, Badger.

About "The Day Joanie Frankenhauser Became a Boy"
"I grew up in the 1950s and '60s, a time when society's idea of mas-culinity and femininity was very narrow. I was a little girl who hated dolls and frilly clothes and who loved climbing trees, throwing a base-ball, and playing Army. Since it seemed I would only be welcomed into my favorite games if I was a boy, I decided to become one. At the age of four, I convinced my parents to cut my hair short, I wore boyish clothes, and I insisted on being called Tommy. Of course, everyone knew I was actually a girl pretending to be a boy (a "tomboy," as girls

like me were called). I couldn't hide because in those days, girls had to wear dresses to school. If I was growing up now, when girls are allowed to go to school in shorts and T-shirts, I might actually be able to pass as a boy for an extended period of time. It was imagining what I would see and do and learn as a faux boy that led me to write 'The Day Joanie Frankenhauser Became a Boy.' "

DONNA JO NAPOLI has published over forty books for preschoolers through high schoolers. *The Prince of the Pond* won the New Jersey Reading Association Award. *Stones in Water* won the Sydney Taylor Award and the Golden Kite Award. *Albert* won the Kentucky Blue Grass Award. Ms. Napoli received the Drexel University/Free Library of Philadelphia Citation for Excellence in Children's Literature. She is a professor of linguistics and the mother of five.

About "Twelve"

"I was a tomboy and my mother feared I'd never be feminine enough to be successful as a woman. (In her eyes that meant getting married and having children.) The poem is personal in a way that my fiction is not."

LINDA SUE PARK is the author of several books for young people, including *A Single Shard,* winner of the 2002 Newbery Medal. While she loves to write, she loves to read even more; her first book *(Seesaw Girl)* was based on something she read when she was ten years old! Ms. Park lives in western New York with her husband and two children, and when she grows up, she would like to be an astronaut.

About "The Apple"

"I'm always interested in making things. I love that impulse in people—to create something that can be shared with others, whether it's art or music or writing or craft. I am not a good artist myself, but my father and daughter and husband are, and I love seeing how their work progresses from the first sketches to the final picture or painting. So I wrote this story for them!"

SONYA SONES is the author of three novels-in-verse for readers aged twelve and older: *Stop Pretending, What My Mother Doesn't Know,* and the forthcoming *One of Those Hideous Books Where the Mother Dies.* Before becoming a poet, Ms. Sones was a film animator, taught animation to kids, made films for public television, taught filmmaking at Harvard University, designed baby clothes, and worked as a photographer and a film editor.

About "The Boys in the Bushes"

"I wrote this poem when my poetry teacher, the great Myra Cohn Livingston, asked us to write a poem in iambic pentameter. I had recently visited the neighborhood where I grew up and remembered how the boys used to leap out of the Petersons' bushes and attack us every afternoon on the way home from school. So I decided to write a poem about that."

JUNE RAE WOOD drew on memories of her brother, Richard, to create "Punky," a man with Down syndrome, for her first novel, *The Man Who Loved Clowns.* That book won the Mark Twain Award and the William Allen White Award. More novels followed: *A Share of Freedom, When Pigs Fly, Turtle on a Fence Post,* and *About Face.* Ms. Wood and her husband live near Windsor, Missouri, and have a daughter and two granddaughters.

About "Flying Free"

"I'd been wracking my brain for a short-story idea when one came to me—by Divine Guidance. Well, almost. One Sunday, during his sermon, the minister used an illustration about young eagles learning to fly. That planted the seed, and the idea started to grow. I needed a character who was reluctant to "fly," and a polio victim came to mind. That led me back to my childhood years, when the great polio scare hit my hometown."